A LITTLE SOMETHING EXTRA

Short Stories from the Invertary, Benson Security and Sinclair Sisters worlds

JANET ELIZABETH HENDERSON

ISBN: 978-0-473-50628-5

CONTENTS

A note from the author

Hello,

For some time now, I've been writing a short story each month for my newsletter. It's a chance for everyone to catch up with their favorite characters and for me to tease some things coming up in the Invertary/Benson Security and Sinclair Sisters worlds.

A few months ago, one of my readers suggested that I put these stories together in a book. And I thought that was a great idea—so thank you, Andrew. But I couldn't just use the stories from the newsletter, so I've written eight new ones just for this book. I've arranged the stories in chronological order, so the timeline throughout the book makes sense. There's a note at the top of each story to tell you where it sits in relation to my books.

I hope you enjoy reading these as much as I enjoyed writing them. And if you'd like more short stories, make sure you've signed up for my newsletter.

In the meantime, happy reading!

Janet x

Betty's Birthday

Betty McLeod spent her fiftieth birthday the same way she'd spent every birthday since turning twenty-five. Although, this year was a bit more special than most. It was a double celebration, of sorts—her fiftieth and what would have been her silver wedding anniversary.

"Yer aff yer heid, you know that, right?" Edna McKintyre had been Betty's best friend since primary school, and she was never shy about sharing her opinion. "I managed to get Davy to let me go out for the day, and instead of going tae the shops on Argyll Street, I'm on a bus to the middle of bloody nowhere."

"Auch, haud yer wheisht! We're going to Bearsden, not Timbuktu. When we're done here, there will still be time to get in a bit of shopping. I saw a braw tartan dress in Lewis's that I've had my eye on. I wouldn't mind getting a few of them to see me through."

"Like we're no' Scottish enough without adding everyday tartan to the mix. Why don't you get one of those nice polka dot dresses everybody's wearing?"

"And look like everybody else? No thanks! I'm crafting ma signature style here. I'm looking for something timeless."

"Timeless? Aye, it would have to be, seeing as you're in your fifties now and you've no' got much time left."

"Speak for yourself! I plan to live forever."

"I hear that can happen when you sell your soul to the devil."

"Come on." Betty tugged at her friend's sleeve. "This is our stop." She wriggled out of her seat, making sure not to shuggle the basket she'd carefully packed in Invertary.

They made it to the front of the bus in one piece, just as it screeched to a halt.

"Yer no Stirling Moss, you know that, right?" Betty shouted at the driver as they got off.

He answered by speeding away from the curb.

"Bearsden," Edna said, putting on her poshest accent. "La-de-da. Maybe we should have dressed for the occasion."

The large houses of the newly wealthy lined the wide street, sitting back from the pavement behind well-tended gardens and high hedges.

"Invertary looks better than this."

"Aye, but these people have *money*."

Betty sniffed at the thought. Anyone who was daft enough to think they were better than her because of a few pounds in the bank deserved everything they got.

The house she was looking for was one of the newer builds, with boxy, boring architecture and tiny wee windows. Either the people who bought these houses didn't like daylight, or they were hoping small windows would better deter the burglars. She snorted. *Good luck wae that.* In some areas of Glasgow, robbing a Bearsden house was a rite of passage.

"This is the one." She pushed through a curlicued gate and strode past a bunch of bored gnomes.

Gnomes. In Bearsden. And people said she was low class.

"Hurry up," she snapped at Edna.

"I'm coming. I'm coming. Hold yer horses, woman."

"Get the camera out." Betty patted her short hair, which had started to thin—along with the hormones in her system. When a man lost his hair, he was manlier. When a woman lost her hair, she was a crabby old witch. There was no justice in the world—something she'd learned the hard way twenty-five years earlier.

"Make sure you get my best side," Betty told Edna.

"You don't have a best side," Edna muttered.

Betty laughed, flashing teeth that had seen better days—something else she'd no doubt lose along with her hair. With no more delay, she removed the scarf covering her basket, picked up an egg she'd been storing for months just for this day, and lobbed it at the front door.

It made a satisfying splatting noise as it hit, before running down the red paint.

"Bloody hell!" Edna gagged. "How old are those eggs? I'm no' staying here for this. I don't want to puke." With that, she ran back down the path.

"You'd better have taken that picture," Betty shouted after her. She needed it to round out her scrapbook.

With evil delight, she took another egg from her basket and aimed for the pristine windows. It was worth suffering the smell to see the result.

"Stop that right now!" The shout came from the back of the property. "I'm calling the police this time. I've had enough."

"Aye, it's only been twenty-five years," Betty said to the person who ran into the front garden. "I can see where your patience would be wearing a bit thin." She threw another egg and smiled when it hit.

"Betty McLeod, you're a nasty, bitter old woman."

Betty turned to the woman she'd once trusted more than anyone. "And you're a flabby old slag. How many spare tires is that around your waist now? Four?"

"Get off ma property. Go find something else to do with your life instead of annoying me."

"I do plenty with my life. This just happens to be my annual highlight." She threw another egg.

"Haven't you had enough revenge? It was a mistake. I told you that. I'm not even with him anymore. I haven't been with him for twenty-four bloody years." Hands on hips, she confronted Betty and glared at her. "I did you a favor. He was a bastard. You would have been miserable with him."

"You're probably right. But I never got the chance to find out for myself, because you went to bed with him the week before the wedding."

"You didn't miss anything," Maureen said. "He was rubbish in bed."

"Another thing I never got to find out." She lobbed two eggs at the same time for that cheek. "You always were a jealous wee cow. Always wanting everything I got my hands on. What was the matter, Mo, did you figure out that you'd always be in my shadow, no matter what you did?"

Maureen snorted. "You're delusional. Maw was right about you. You're going to waste your whole life because you can't let go of the past. You're going to die a lonely, bitter old woman, Betty McLeod."

"Better than a two-faced, man-stealing, easy-with-her-favors old hag, Maureen McLeod."

"That's it." Betty's younger sister threw up her hands in disgust. Drama queen. "I'm done with this. Have at it. Throw your eggs. I don't care. You're the one who's missing out. You're the one who has family you never see. Nieces and nephews you've never met. And all because Ramsay

4

MacDonald had wandering hands. It's pathetic. You're pathetic."

"It wasnae only his hands that wandered though, was it?" Betty was running out of eggs. "And it wandered all over my own sister. I don't know how you can live with yourself."

"It's easy. Because you're no' here to drive me mad!"

Damn it. She'd run out of eggs. But—she smirked at the house—she'd still managed to make a good job of decorating for her birthday.

"I'm done," Betty said. "See you next year."

"Ha! That's where you're mistaken. We won't be here. Paul got a job in the States."

That made Betty pause. She might hate her sister with a vengeance, but America was awfully far away. It would be a helluva trip to make with two dozen rotten eggs.

"Where in America?"

"Like I'd tell you!" Maureen turned her back on Betty. "Enjoy your sad, lonely life without me. I know I'll be living it up without you." She disappeared back around the side of the house, and Betty wished she'd kept a few eggs to throw at her sister.

"You're dead to me," she shouted after her, but it wasn't up to the standard of her usual retorts.

"Feeling better?" Edna said when Betty met up with her on the pavement outside the house.

"I was, until Mo told me she's moving to America." Betty wanted to hit something at the thought. "How am I supposed to get my birthday vengeance now?"

Edna linked her arm with Betty's. "Maybe it's time to move on. You've had twenty-five good years."

Betty let out a heavy sigh. "I'm still right pissed off with her."

"But no' with Ramsay, I see." It was a long-standing argument between them.

"You can get over a man's betrayal, but a sister should always be on *your* side." She thought about it. "She's dead to me. I am now, officially, family free."

"You, Betty McLeod, are a deeply disturbed individual."

There was no arguing with that. "Let's get a pie at City Bakeries. Then we can go to the department store and see that tartan dress."

They headed toward the bus stop, arm in arm, as gray clouds gathered over Glasgow. Betty took some satisfaction in knowing that the rich folk got the bad weather, just like the rest of them.

"Have you ever noticed," Edna said, "that rotten eggs smell a lot like sulfur?"

Betty smiled with satisfaction. Her nickname wasn't Satan for nothing.

It Wisnae Me

"I'm designing my own knickers," Betty announced to the Domino Boys as she stalked into the community center.

The old men were gathered around their usual table, pretending to play dominoes. Really, their games were just an excuse to get together and gossip. It was pathetic. Betty didn't gossip. That was nothing more than spreading *other* people's news. Betty preferred to make her own.

"Is there a reason you're telling us this?" Archie McPherson said as he reached for the chocolate biscuits.

Betty shoved his hand out of the way and nabbed the last two. "I figured if Kirsty can design underwear, then so can I. I've got a lot more experience than she does, and I've discovered a gap in the market. There's no sexy underwear for your discerning oldie. I'm making knickers for people our age."

"Still no' sure why you're telling us this." Archie scowled at the biscuits in her hand.

She took a bite of one and grinned while she chewed, thankful she'd remembered to put her teeth in this time. "I'm starting with designs for men because their underwear is less complicated. And I need models," she said with her mouth full. "That's why I'm here. To ask if you want to model my underwear."

Hamish spat his tea over the table, and James thumped him on the back. Findlay looked like she'd asked them to lay an egg.

"You're aff yer heid if you think I'm going tae strut around in my underpants for you," James said.

Betty nodded sagely. "That's what the Drymen Domino Team said you'd say."

"Drymen?" Hamish sat up straight. "You've been talking to the Drymen men?"

"It just so happens I bumped into Charlie MacDonald at the post office a couple of hours ago. He's up visiting his nephew. He thought the underwear was a great idea." She rubbed her chin. "He even mentioned making a calendar and raising some money for their club. Of course, I said that I needed to offer the option to the Invertary team first. To keep it local, you understand. But he said you lot were too chicken to pose in your underwear." She shrugged and turned away. "Nae skin aff ma nose. I've got my models."

She'd barely taken three steps before Archie piped up, "Now wait a wee minute. You can't get the Drymen boys to model underwear designed in Invertary. We keep that stuff in-house. After Kirsty and Lake's fashion show, people expect the folk of Invertary to know about underwear. And we're no' ashamed to be part of a local endeavor, are we boys?"

There was a chorus of agreement. Swallowing her smile, Betty turned back to them. "I don't know. The Drymen boys are a wee bit younger. They'll probably sell more underwear."

James frowned at her. "I thought you said this underwear of yours was aimed at folk our age. Ones in their seventies and eighties?"

"Aye," she said.

"Then what the hell are you doing going after younger models?"

"To be fair, the Drymen boys are only in their sixties. Which means they can probably pull off sexy a wee bit better than you four can," Betty said.

"I can do sexy." Findlay struck a pose that she assumed was meant as proof of his claim. It just looked like there was something stuck in his dentures and his tongue was working it out.

"You're right." Betty kept a straight face. "You're definitely what I need. And it would be good to keep it local. Those Drymen boys are awfy full o' themselves anyway."

"Wait a minute," Archie said. "How do we know you're telling the truth about the Drymen Team wanting to model for you?"

The men nodded their agreement.

"If you don't believe me, go catch Charlie. He's at the pub. He'll tell you." There was no need to pull off another innocent look; for once she was telling the truth. Charlie would indeed back up her story.

"She wouldn't say that if it wasn't true," James said.

"You really do have Drymen interested in this?" Hamish said.

"Well," Betty conceded, "they've no' signed on the dotted line because I wanted to ask you lot first."

They shared a look.

"We cannae let Drymen best us," James said.

"No," Archie said, then looked at Betty. "You've got yourself some models."

"Great," Betty said, "I've got a photographer all lined up. Be at this address at seven tonight."

She put a piece of paper in front of them on the table, and Archie picked it up.

"That's the cemetery," he said, looking even more confused than usual.

"Aye, what better place for a fashion shoot aimed at oldies than their next destination?"

"I don't see what's sexy about a bunch of graves," Findlay said.

"Just be there on time. I know what I'm doing, and I brought in some experts to help." With that, she tottered out of the room.

As soon as she was through the swing doors and out into the street, she spotted Charlie MacDonald.

"How'd it go?" he said.

"Mission accomplished. Got them all signed up." Betty grinned at him. "Guess that means I owe you a pie and a pint."

"That you do." He chuckled.

❧

IT WAS DARK IN THE CEMETERY, BUT YOU WOULDN'T HAVE known it from the amount of light coming from Betty McLeod's memorial statue. The one she'd had commissioned for when she died. It showed Mel Gibson from *Braveheart* carrying a replica of Betty in his arms. The statue had cost an arm and a leg but was worth every penny.

"Is this what you wanted?" Claire Donaldson said as she finished setting up the lights that they'd hired in Fort William.

Betty cast a critical eye over the scene she'd paid the teenagers to set up. With strategic lighting and the fog coming from the dry-ice machine, the graveyard looked like a movie set.

"What's the name of that singer?" she said. "Could only

afford one glove. Sometimes he was black. Sometimes he was white."

"Michael Jackson," the twins said at the same time.

"Aye." Betty nodded. "This looks like that video he did. The one with Vincent Price talking at the start of it." She let out a dreamy sigh. "Now that was a sexy man."

"Michael Jackson?" Claire asked.

"Don't be daft. Vincent Price." Kids these days didn't know anything. "Have you got the sheep?"

Megan pointed toward the fence where five stolen sheep were tethered. The sheep didn't care that they were out of their usual paddock, or that it was dark, or that they'd been dyed pastel shades for the event. No, all the sheep cared about was that the grass was nice and thick and there were plenty of flowers on the graves to munch on.

"Once we start shooting, we'll let them go so they can wander in amongst the graves," Betty said.

"I don't think that's a good idea," Megan said. "Sheep are pretty dumb. The chances of them staying where you want them are slim. And I don't want to chase them down again. It took ages to catch them." She looked at her twin. "I think they're onto us. They see us coming and run. It's like they know we're going to dye them."

Claire nodded. "We need to keep them tied up."

"No." Betty was adamant. "I need them to wander. It's going tae add atmosphere."

The young lassies didn't look convinced, but this was her photo shoot, not theirs. And she knew what she was doing.

"Are you sure this is legal?" Claire said.

Betty cocked an eyebrow at her. "More legal than stealing Kitty Baxter's sheep."

"Borrowed. We borrowed them. You said you wanted sheep. How else were we supposed to get them?"

"We're not getting paid enough for this," Megan added. "If our brother finds out we've been dyeing sheep again, he's going to lock us up in his cell. And this time, he won't let us out."

"We need to move to a town where we aren't related to the only local cop," Claire said.

"Amen sister," Megan muttered.

"I'm here, I'm here," Jean called out as she rushed into the graveyard. "Sorry I'm late. The Knit or Die meeting ran over time. Now, what am I taking photos of? Oh, look at the pretty sheep."

Betty fought the urge to roll her eyes. Jean was a dippy as a bag of squirrels, but she owned a good camera.

"I'm waiting for my models," Betty said. "You can aim your camera at my memorial statue. We'll start taking photos there."

"What models?" Jean pulled her camera out of her bag.

"I'm designing underwear. This is the photo shoot for my interweb shop."

"Oh." Jean looked around. "Does Kirsty know about your designs? This isn't another one of your schemes to put her out of business, is it? I'm not allowed to get involved with those anymore. The doctor said my nerves can't handle it. And even if I was involved, I wouldn't be on your side. I owe my allegiance to Knit or Die and they're run by Kirsty's mother. Margaret would kick me out of the club if I helped you interfere with her daughter's lingerie business. And I'm halfway through a blanket. On top of all that, is it even legal to have a fashion shoot in a graveyard?"

Betty held up a hand to stop her talking; otherwise, Jean would just keep going until she ran out of breath. "This isn't illegal." *Mostly.* "And it's got nothing to do with Kirsty." *Mostly.* "And nobody's going tae kick you out of your knitting group." *Probably.* "Now, I thought you wanted to practice taking professional photos. Are you here to do that, or no'?"

Jean nodded. "Okay. As long as you swear this isn't some evil scheme."

"Cross my heart." Betty went through the motions.

Out of the corner of her eye, she saw the twins roll their eyes. At least they were smart enough not to believe a word that came out of her mouth. But then, Jean wasn't known for her brains.

"Good." Jean nodded.

৩

UNDER BETTY'S DIRECTION, THE TWINS HAD STRUNG UP A curtain between two trees so that the men could go behind it to change.

"I'm no' wearing this," came the shout, about ten seconds after she'd handed them the underwear.

"Fine," Betty snapped. "Don't wear it. Twin? Hey, you. Aye, whichever one you are. Hand me my bag. I need my phone if I'm to call the Drymen Domino Team and tell them the modeling's back on."

"You can't just call us twin," Megan told her as she handed Betty her bag. "We have got names."

"You wouldn't dare call Drymen," Archie shouted before his head popped out from behind the curtain.

"Aye, I'd dare." Betty clasped her bag in front of her and glared at him. "If you're no' man enough to model my underwear, then I'll find some men who're up to the challenge."

"These underpants aren't right," he argued.

"They're the latest fashion. I've done my research, and I know what people want. I sold knickers for thirty years. On top of that, Kirsty's Scottish underwear is her best seller. This ties in with that. Now, am I calling Charlie, or are you going to man up and come out from behind the curtain?"

He glared at her, and the curtain dropped back into place.

"Fire up the fog," Betty called to Claire. "Get ready with that camera," she told Jean. "Let the sheep loose as soon as the boys appear," she said to Megan.

They were ready. Holding her breath, she waited for the men to come out from behind the curtain. The material twitched. There was muttering. Someone cursed. And then the curtain was whipped back. Three of the four old men who called themselves the Domino Boys stepped out into the graveyard.

Claire gasped. Megan sounded like she was choking. And Jean's jaw dropped.

Betty grinned.

The men were naked except for the underpants she'd provided and their socks and shoes. But it wasn't the wrinkles or the pasty white skin that had the women stunned—it was the underwear.

"This looks daft," Archie said, pointing at the sporran stuck to the front of his tartan briefs. "And it's no' very practical."

As a pink sheep wandered past him, Betty remembered the camera. "Get snapping, Jean. We don't want to miss any of this."

"Aye." Jean sounded a bit stunned, but she took the photos.

"The underwear isn't supposed to be practical," Betty told Archie. "It's supposed to be modern and sexy. And it is. Isn't it twins?"

"Oh, aye, dead sexy," Claire said in a high-pitched voice.

Megan just kept on choking.

"At least you've got a sporran," James complained. "All I've got is this patch of tartan to cover my goods, and my arse is hanging out." He turned around, and sure enough, his bum cheeks were bare, and there was a string up the middle of his backside. Well, two strings.

Megan made a strangled noise, while her sister just gawked.

"It's called a jock strap," Betty told him. "I looked it up. But you're wearing it wrong. Those straps are supposed to go around your thighs, not up your backside."

"Then there would be nothing there at all." James sounded affronted. "This is indecent. I could get arrested flashing my arse like this."

"It's supposed to be sexy," Betty reminded him. "For the boudoir."

"Even if I was inclined to get frisky in this thing, by the time I got it off, the mood would have passed."

"Just go drape yourself over a gravestone while Jean takes some photos."

"I'm no' sitting on one. No' with my backside hanging out." James stomped over to a headstone, followed by a pale blue sheep.

"What's this thing?" Hamish said, pointing at the little tartan apron covering his privates. Under it, he had on white Y-fronts.

"It's a loin cloth," Betty said. "And why are you still wearing your underwear?"

"I'm no' wearing this thing on its own." Hamish stared down at it. "This is very wrong."

"No' as wrong as this," Findlay said as he came out from behind the curtain.

At the sight of him, Megan let out a high-pitched whine and clutched the fence. She kept her face averted, but her shoulders were shaking.

"That's no' technically underwear," Betty said. "It's part of my swimwear line. That's a mankini. In Royal Tartan."

"I don't care what you call it," Findlay said. "It looks like a G-string with suspenders attached. No self-respecting man would be seen dead in this." He tugged at one of the straps that ran from the pouch covering his privates, up his chest, and over his shoulders.

"He's got a point," Archie said. "I don't see your designs selling. They're nowhere near sexy. In fact, you could market them as birth control. One look at your man in these and you'd never want to do the deed ever again."

"Stop whining and pose. We've no' got all night. I'm hiring that fog machine by the hour, and the twins here need to get Kitty's sheep back before she notices they're missing." Although, their dye job might clue the woman in that they'd taken a wee trip away from her farm.

Hamish shook his head. "I'm no' doing this. I look like an idiot. I'll never live it down."

The other men nodded, and Betty knew she was losing them.

"Just give me one minute," she said. "I've got a photo of a runway show on my computer phone that will prove this is the height of fashion."

She dug her phone out of her massive black handbag and pressed its buttons. While the men complained, Jean took photos, and the twins tried to hide their laughter, Betty muttered at her phone. The thing was damn hard to work, and the buttons were fiddly, but she eventually managed to call the number she wanted—because there were no fashion show photos on her phone.

"I'm freezing my balls off here," Hamish said. "Literally. I don't have a minute to give you."

"I cannae find the photos anyway." Because they didn't exist. "How about you just do a couple of poses, and then we'll call it a night?" She stuffed her phone back into her handbag.

"No," Archie said. "I don't want my photo out in the world dressed like this. Get the Drymen boys to model your stuff. They deserve it. And make sure to delete all the photos you've taken tonight."

He turned toward the curtain.

That's when the flashing lights hit the graveyard entrance. And then the siren wailed.

For a second, nobody moved.

And then it was pure chaos.

The men ran every which way. Hamish hid behind a gravestone, and Archie tried to climb a tree. The scared sheep darted about in confusion, baaing continually. The yellow one knocked James off his feet, and he landed on his back in front of a headstone, flowers around his head. Megan jumped the fence and ran for it. Claire dithered, first running for the sheep, then running to help James, then deciding it would be best to scarper. She was too late. Her brother's police car screeched to a halt in front of her, blocking her escape. In the midst of all this, Findlay had pulled down the curtain and wrapped himself in it. And Betty hadn't moved.

Because she'd been the one to call the cops.

With clear resignation, Matt Donaldson climbed from his police car. "Please tell me this isn't some weird geriatric Satanic ritual," he said.

"I think I slipped a disk," James said from the grave. "I can't move."

A green sheep stopped in front of the cop car and peed. Matt looked at the sheep, then at his younger sister who was looking anywhere but at him. Then his eyes landed on Betty.

She lifted her hands, palms up. "What?" she demanded. "Whatever it is, it wisnae me."

And then she threw back her head and cackled. The underwear she'd purchased from that dodgy sex clothes catalog she'd found stuffed into her letterbox had been worth every penny.

Quickly, before Matt could confiscate it, she snatched

Jean's camera from her hands. "I'm going home," she announced. And then, she headed out of the graveyard.

"Get back here, Betty McLeod," Matt shouted. But he had his hands full, so he wasn't about to chase her down anytime soon.

Betty pulled her phone from her bag and hit the button to call Harry—the computer genius who was old enough to buy beer, but still liked playing with Lego. For some reason, Harry always assumed the best about Betty. It was weird. But he was in town visiting his mother, which made him the perfect choice to help her.

"Harry, son," Betty said. "I need to get some photos off a camera and put them on the interweb. Can you help me with that? It has to be done straight away. I'm on a tight schedule here."

"Of course I can help," Harry said. "What website do you want to put them on?"

Her smile turned evil as she stared out across the black waters of the loch.

"The one Kirsty has for her lingerie shop," she said, and then she started laughing.

Jena and Matt's Honeymoon in Vegas

"I feel like we've landed right into the middle of every Hollywood cliché," Matt Donaldson said as he looked out of their hotel window.

Arms snaked around his waist from behind. "Stop complaining," his wife said. "It's Vegas, baby!"

It was indeed. Beneath them, the famous Strip bustled with people, so many of them at times, Matt wondered why they weren't tripping over each other.

"How the hell do they police this?" His cop brain spun with the dynamics of keeping the city safe for residents and tourists alike.

"Well," Jena said as she slid around to his front. "They have more than one cop for a start." She beamed up at him, her hair wild around her shoulders, evidence that they'd spent the day in bed. "Is my small-town man freaking out over the big city?"

"I hate to break it to you, Princess, but this isn't a city. This is Disney for deviants."

She smacked her palm in the middle of his chest. "Stop

being such a stick-in-the-mud. We're here to have fun. You need to loosen up and relax."

Yeah, that wasn't going to happen. Maybe if they'd honeymooned on a desert island, he'd be able to relax. But here? Impossible. Everywhere he looked there was something that made him want to arrest someone. So far, he'd spotted two guys selling something illegal from the back of their car, at least three hookers working the tourist crowd, and a pickpocket making a mint from people while they watched the Bellagio fountains. And that was only the stuff he'd seen on the trip from the airport to the hotel.

"I know when you look out the window all you see is the seedier side of things," Jena said, "but try to see it through my eyes."

She turned to face the window and leaned back into him. Automatically, he wrapped his arms around her and held her tight. It'd only been a few short months since he'd almost lost her, and he never passed up on an opportunity to hold her close and remind himself she was alive and well.

And his.

"All those sparkly lights," Jena said, "and the over-the-top hotels are like Christmas decorations. They make me feel like all I have to do is set foot outside the door, and I'll have an adventure. And the people? They're just like us. They've sacrificed and saved so they can come have fun for a few days in a place that sparkles everywhere they turn. They've pored over the events websites, getting excited about which show they're going to catch and which restaurant they'll eat in, or which tacky tourist thing they'll see first. And then, when they're standing in front of the tackiest tourist attraction, they'll grin at everyone around them, knowing they're all in on the joke together. Because, we know it's tacky, but for this vacation, we're going to let ourselves enjoy it anyway. *You* see people getting conned, but I see people trying new things, stepping out of their comfort zones, letting their hair down and having some fun."

Matt buried his face in her throat and nuzzled her soft skin, breathing her scent deep into his lungs and filling himself with her. "Don't worry, Princess, I won't get in the way of your fun." He also wouldn't stop noticing the cons, but he'd keep the observations to himself.

"*Our* fun," she said firmly as she arched her neck for him.

"Our fun," he agreed as he nibbled behind her ear, making her shiver in his arms.

"You need to stop doing that, or we won't get out of this hotel room." But she wiggled her curvy backside against him while she protested.

"That doesn't sound like such a bad idea."

Jena made a sound that was partway between encouragement and protest. "We've been in here all day. Not that I'm complaining, but the town's just waking up, and I'm hungry."

"We could call room service." He nipped at her shoulder.

"Matt," she complained, half-heartedly for sure, but it was still a complaint. "I want to show you something of my life before I moved to Scotland. I can't do that from a hotel room."

"Princess, you were a go-go dancer in Atlantic City. This is Las Vegas."

"And we couldn't go to Atlantic City because of that mob thing."

He worked to relax his suddenly tense muscles. *That mob thing* was her ex-boyfriend trying to blow up half of Scotland to get her back.

"Plus," she said. "Where's the fun in honeymooning in your hometown? Here, I can give you the club experience I helped create in Atlantic City. Only, no mob. Trust me, it will be great. You're going to have a blast."

No. He wasn't. But he was going to grit his teeth and make sure *she* had a blast.

"Fine." He sighed. "Get ready and we'll leave."

"Yay!" Standing on tiptoe, she wrapped her arms around his neck and kissed him hard. "Don't worry. If you hate anything, we can come back here." And with that, she darted to the bathroom.

Matt watched her cute ass sway in sexy white lingerie, the long golden curls of her hair skimming her hips. Man, she was gorgeous. A slow smile curved his lips. She was also his. As she disappeared into the bathroom to spend about four years on her makeup, Matt looked down at his brand-new wedding ring. He'd put aside his discomfort and make their trip one to remember. It was the least he could do.

For his wife.

৩৶৩

HOURS LATER, MATT GRITTED HIS TEETH AS JENA MURDERED Adele's 'Hello' on the stage of a karaoke bar on the Strip. They'd been walking through one of the casinos, surrounded by slot machines with their flashing lights and ringing bells, when Jena had pointed to a dark corner of the vast room and squealed. The next thing he knew, he was being dragged into a seedy bar so she could sing on stage. Or, try to sing.

There was no denying, his wife was made for the spotlight. From her voluptuous curves to her long legs—made even longer by her mile-high sparkly stripper shoes—she oozed sex appeal. Add in her stunning face, those big eyes of hers, and all that long, wavy hair, and every man in the place was drooling. Which pissed him off big time.

Fortunately, Jena's singing went a long way toward killing any fantasies the audience might have.

"I can't take anymore," someone called out. "Get her off the stage!"

The crowd was turning as Jena wailed to the backing music. People mumbled. One or two heckled. It was only a matter of time before Jena noticed and then she'd be all sad eyes and pouting lips. There was only one way to prevent that from happening. With a sigh, he climbed onto the stage beside her.

She beamed at him but appeared confused when he took the mic from her hand. When a cheer went up, Jena frowned at the audience.

"What's going on?" she whispered at him.

"Excuse us," he said into the mic. "We're changing things up a little. I'm going to sing, and my lovely wife is going to dance."

There was a mixed reaction from the crowd. Cheers. Boos. Mainly indifference.

Jena covered the mic with her hand. "Why are you stopping my song? I was doing great."

"I want to show off your dancing," he half lied. She *was* a killer dancer. "And I want to do this with you." That was a full lie. He'd rather have his nails removed with pliers than sing in front of a crowd.

She gave him a look filled with such love that he felt ten foot tall. "Can you sing, though? This crowd's tough. I don't want them to turn on you. Maybe I should keep singing, and you should dance."

Man, he loved his clueless woman. He squeezed her shoulder. "Princess, you've seen my dancing. Trust me when I say, my singing is better. Anyway, they won't be listening to me; they'll be too busy watching you dance."

She bit her lower lip and glanced at the restless crowd. "Okay. If you're sure."

"I'm sure." He cued up their song. "We're doing one of Josh's numbers. If you tell him about this, I'm divorcing you."

With a giggle, Jena faced the crowd. "Let's knock them dead."

The crowd groaned when the music started. Matt ignored them and kept his eyes on Jena. She'd already started dancing, and it was mesmerizing. Sexy, fluid perfection. It made him want to take her back to the hotel and make use of the Californian king size in their suite. He was so focused on watching her that he almost missed his cue, which earned him another heckle.

Then he started singing, and it was Jena's turn to stumble. She stared at him wide-eyed as he put the years of singing lessons his mother had forced him to take as a kid to good use. The same singing lessons he'd had to pay his sisters never to mention to a soul—especially Josh McInnes.

When their song ended, the crowd cheered and whistled. Some of them even got to their feet.

Jena threw herself into his arms. "We need to go on *America's Got Talent*," she shouted over the noise.

And Matt burst out laughing.

⚜

They'd eaten dinner at the Hard Rock Cafe and stocked up on snacks at Hershey's Chocolate World. They'd joined the crowds to watch the pirate ship battle outside Treasure Island, the volcano erupt outside The Mirage, and the fountains dance to a Celine Dion song outside the Bellagio. They'd sung in a Karaoke bar, played the slots in Caesar's Palace, and taken a strange walk among pink flamingoes living in an indoor park in the appropriately named Flamingo casino.

Now, they were in a nightclub where one of Jena's friends

from Atlantic City worked as a go-go dancer. And Matt was beginning to think he didn't have the energy to keep up with his wife. Because, although she was still jumping around, all he wanted to do was go to bed and sleep for a week.

"So, this is what middle age feels like," he said to a guy standing next to him at the bar.

"Long night?" the guy said as his large, and clearly armed friend watched them closely.

The guy's bespoke suit and the fact that he was traveling with a bodyguard screamed wealth and entitlement, making Matt wonder if he was chatting to a celebrity. Not a famous one, obviously, because Matt didn't have a clue who he was.

He mentally shrugged before answering the man, "Aye, long night." He gestured to one of the massive glowing cubes set up around the darkened room. Jena and her friend were dancing on top of it as it changed colors with the beat. "And it's going to get longer. My woman doesn't look anywhere near calling it quits."

"Which one's yours?" The guy turned and leaned back against the bar as he sipped his drink. His bodyguard stepped forward to keep the crowd away from him.

"The one wearing the sparkly stilts." He grinned, wondering again how his wife walked in her shoes.

"You're a lucky man," the guy said, with speculation in his voice.

"Aye," Matt said, his eyes on Jena.

A glance around the crowded dance floor told him that his eyes weren't the only ones on his wife. And he didn't like the leers some of her admirers were sending her way. It was time to position himself beside her platform.

"Nice talking to you," he said as he stepped away from the bar.

"I'll give you fifty grand for her," the guy in the suit said, stopping Matt in his tracks.

"What the hell?" Matt said.

The man eyed him with calculation. "Eighty grand."

It was as though he'd slipped into an alternate dimension. The dance floor was still crowded, the music still blared, and the lights still flashed in the darkness. He had to be losing his mind. Because this conversation was at odds with everything he knew to be real.

"Eighty grand," the man repeated. "All you have to do is walk away right now and let me step in with your woman."

"Have you lost your mind? You can't buy a woman," Matt said. "And I can't sell her. I don't bloody own her."

The guy cocked his head. "You said she was your woman."

Matt held up his left hand. "My wife," he snapped.

The man nodded slowly. "A hundred and twenty."

"Are you even listening to me?" he demanded, and the bodyguard took a menacing step closer. "You don't buy women."

The man shrugged like this was a normal occurrence. And maybe it was for him. Who knew? It was bloody surreal for Matt. "Is this one of those prank reality TV shows?" he asked, trying to make sense of the situation.

"No." The man gave him a tight-lipped smile. "I just know what I want and how to get it." His eyes hardened. "I'm used to getting what I want."

"Well, you aren't getting my wife."

"Five hundred thousand," the asshole said.

"You could offer billions, and I still wouldn't sell her. A, because she isn't a possession that I can sell. And B, because selling people is against the law." With a disgusted shake of his head, Matt turned to stalk away.

A meaty hand on his shoulder halted him. "Boss ain't done," the bodyguard said.

"Aye, he is." Matt shrugged off the guy's hold and headed for his wife.

He'd taken no more than three steps before the body-guard blocked his path and the rich asshole stepped in front of him.

"One million dollars and you walk away, leaving the blonde with me." He looked Matt up and down, assessing, quite rightly, that he wasn't rolling in money. "All you need to do is hand your account details to my associate here." He motioned to the meathead.

He was clearly off his head, and Matt had had enough of dealing with him. "Get out of my way. We're done here."

A hand tightened on his upper arm, holding him in place. He glared up at the bodyguard. "Let. Go."

The crowd danced around them, the deafening music and flashing lights making it hard to focus. A staff member appeared at their sides, as though he'd materialized out of thin air.

"Is everything okay, Mr. Shepherd?" he asked the asshole trying to buy Matt's wife.

"It will be," Shepherd said, his eyes still on Matt.

"What the hell?" Matt said as the hold tightened on his left arm. "Everything isn't okay. This guy is trying to buy my wife from me like we're in some crap Hollywood movie." He glared at Shepherd. "Let me tell you, you're no Redford."

The staff member paled, obviously unsure of what to do next.

Matt relieved him of his indecision. "Call the cops," he ordered. "Get them here fast. Because things are about to get out of control." With that, he pulled back his arm and punched Shepherd in the face.

He was right. Pandemonium ensued. The bodyguard grabbed him from behind. The club staffer ran for the bar. Women screamed. Shepherd aimed a punch at Matt, but he ducked, and it hit the bodyguard. An alarm sounded. People ran for the exits. Matt ignored it all as he broke the bodyguard's hold, turned, and kicked the asshole in the balls. When he doubled over, Matt snatched the gun from his shoulder holster and aimed it at Shepherd, who stopped dead in his tracks and raised his hands.

"I think we'll wait for the cops," Matt said as Jena screeched his name.

⁂

"I don't understand how you police this city," Matt told the cop taking his statement. "I've been here less than forty-eight hours and have seen more laws broken in that time than I did in two years policing Glasgow."

"It helps when the tourists don't pull guns on the local mob." The cop grinned at him.

"To be fair"—Matt reached for one of the donuts in the box on the detective's desk—"it wasn't my gun."

"Don't touch the donuts," Jena ordered from beside him. "I bought them for the police officers."

"I *am* a police officer," Matt pointed out.

"Not in this country." Jena frowned at him. "I can't believe you started a fight in the nightclub. And aimed a gun at someone. This is our honeymoon."

"Princess, he was trying to buy you."

She rolled her eyes at him. "Like I would have gone with him even if you did sell me."

"What are you talking about? Do you honestly think I'd try to sell you?"

"Of course not. I was just pointing out that it wouldn't be a legal sale if I didn't agree to it. Which means I wouldn't have gone with him."

Matt shook his head to clear it. "Princess, it wouldn't have been a legal sale whether you'd gone along with it or not. And I seriously hope you wouldn't even consider being sold. You wouldn't, right?" He paused, waiting for her reaction.

She just rolled her eyes at him, like he was asking something stupid. Yet again, things had been lost in translation with his wife.

Matt carried on talking, hoping to make his point clear. "I took his bodyguard's gun to stop him using it against us. His boss wouldn't take no for an answer. I was worried they'd take you at gunpoint."

She put a hand on his shoulder. "Don't be silly; you wouldn't have let them do that."

"Exactly. That's what I was doing. Stopping them from taking you."

"Oh," Jena said.

Matt pinched the bridge of his nose while the detective grinned at them.

"Do you see what I'm dealing with here?" Matt asked.

"What?" Jena demanded.

"Okay," the detective said. "I think we've got everything we need. You two can go back to your hotel." She gave them a rueful smile. "You might want to avoid the clubs for the rest of your stay."

"Three more days," Matt said as he looked at his wife. "I'm thinking hotel room and room service for the duration."

She leaned into his side, resting her head on his shoulder. "That sounds perfect. Although, maybe we could take a gondola trip around the shops, seeing as we're staying in the Venetian."

Matt stroked her back while he looked at the detective. "What are the chances of someone trying to buy her in the Venetian shopping mall?"

"Slim," she said with a smile.

"Then we can have a gondola ride," Matt said as he kissed his wife's head.

"I can't believe that creep's top offer for me was only a million dollars," Jena said. "I'm worth way more than that. Hell, Robert Redford paid a million for Demi Moore in the nineties. Even with inflation, we'd be looking at two million today. Right?" She looked up at Matt.

"Princess"—he shook his head at her—"you're priceless."

"I know, right?" She buried her face in his chest as Matt tried not to chuckle.

"You want a ride back to the hotel?" the cop asked.

"Thanks," Matt said. "I think that would be safest."

"No kidding," the woman muttered as she reached for her phone.

"Do you know the worst part?" Jena said, sounding sleepy.

"What's the worst part?" He pulled her closer.

"I left my bag of Hershey's goodies at the nightclub."

All Matt could do was grin and hold his wife tight. But Jena wasn't done. She angled her face up at him.

"Still the best honeymoon ever, right?"

"Absolutely," he said.

And then he kissed his wife.

Andrew McInnes' Book Club

Helen McInnes, Caroline McInnes, Jena Donaldson, and Abby Boyle tiptoed up to the conservatory at the back of Caroline's castle.

"They're going to see us," Helen, Caroline's mother-in-law, hissed.

"No, they won't." Caroline pointed to the group of large ceramic pots with ornamental trees. "I had the gardeners group all of the pots in the darkest part of the patio. Then I opened the little window behind the blinds so we can hear them better."

"Didn't Josh wonder why all the plants were suddenly in one spot?" Helen asked.

"I told him it made it easier to trim the trees to match," Caroline said.

"He believed that?"

Caroline just patted her hand and gave her a pitying look. Her son wasn't known for thinking things through, but Caroline didn't want to shatter his mother's delusions.

There was a scrape and thump from behind them.

"Will you try to walk quieter?" she told Abby. "They're going to hear us."

"I'm four thousand months pregnant with twins," Abby said with a glare. "You try being quiet when your center of gravity shifts two feet in front of you. I can't even see my feet. I have no idea where I'm stepping. This is as quiet as it's going to get."

"I'm pregnant too, and I can lift my feet when I walk."

"You're six months pregnant with one tiny baby. You barely have a bump. I'm having two freaking elephants, and they're due any minute. It's a miracle I can stand up without toppling over."

"Maybe we should carry her?" Caroline said to her mother-in-law.

They stopped at the edge of the patio and the three women eyed the very pregnant brunette.

"I'm not sure we can lift her," Jena said.

"I hate every single of one of you," Abby said.

"Would it make you feel better if you knew I also had the gardeners move the bench behind the plants so we can sit down?" Caroline said.

"Marginally." Abby waddled up the steps and onto the patio. "Come on. If we don't hurry, the men will come into the conservatory and see us. Then they'll know we aren't on a girls' night out." And then she moved slower than a snail. "Although, as girls' nights out go, this one sucks."

"Trust me," Caroline told her. "It will get better."

Abby just muttered something under her breath about making everyone suffer if it didn't.

"How can you walk so silently in those shoes?" Helen eyed Jena's ten-inch platform sandals. This pair was sparkly pink with diamanté detailing on the ankle straps.

"I could run up a mountain in these," Jena whispered. "Sometimes I wear them to work. If I'm plastering a wall or something that makes being taller handy, the height really comes in useful. I just cover them with plastic wrap to them to stop them getting dirty."

Helen stumbled, and Caroline shot out a hand to steady her. "You do construction work in those shoes?"

Jena tossed her long honey-colored hair over her shoulder and nodded. "I like wearing them with my Daisy Dukes and a tartan shirt tied tight under my boobs. It's comfortable and practical."

"And looks like some guy's idea of a porn plot—stripper does DIY," Abby grumbled.

Jena patted her best friend's back and gave her a compassionate smile. "Pregnancy really brings out your evil side, doesn't it?"

"I know!" Abby's eyes filled with tears. "I feel like I'm possessed by the spirit of Betty."

"I think she'd have to die first for that to happen," Jena said.

"Can we focus?" Caroline said. "We need to hurry up, or they'll spot us." She grabbed Abby's arm. "You get the other one," she said to Jena.

And with that, they half-dragged Abby to the bench.

"This is what I miss most when we're back in Atlantic City," Helen said. "Our girls' nights out back home usually involve getting the early bird at the local diner." She shook her head in disgust. "Those women don't know how to live."

"And we do?" Abby said. "We're sitting on a cold wooden bench, behind a bunch of potted trees, waiting to spy on our husbands."

"Honey," Helen drawled, "trust me when I say, if you'd ever eaten the early bird at Jack's Diner, you'd know you were living it up right now."

"Jack's Diner?" Jena said. "I used to eat there after the clubs closed. Their food's fine if you don't go early evening.

They don't salt the early bird special on account of all the old people with heart problems. It's like eating cardboard."

"See?" Helen pointed at Jena.

The women were just getting settled when the men appeared in the kitchen beyond the conservatory.

"They're getting snacks," Helen said. "We should have brought snacks."

"Which reminds me," Jena whispered as she opened her oversized leather handbag and pulled out a bottle of wine. "Cheers," she said with a grin. She unscrewed the cap and took a gulp before handing the bottle to Helen.

Helen stared at it for a moment, shrugged then had a drink too.

"What about me?" Abby whined. "I can't drink. And neither can Caroline. Not that she usually drinks, but we shouldn't miss out just because our dumbass husbands knocked us up."

Jena reached back into her bag and came out with two small tubs of Belgian chocolate ice cream and two spoons. "It's a bit soft," she said as she handed one each to Caroline and Abby.

"You carry ice cream in your handbag?" Helen whispered in awe.

"Not all the time," Jena said, reaching for the wine.

"I don't understand," Abby said. "Why are we watching our men watch a game? I was promised a night out. This isn't a night out. I already do this at home. Every time I walk into the living room, Flynn is talking Katy through yet another football game. I don't need to hear that crap from other women's husbands too."

"Pregnancy really does dull the brain," Jena said. "They aren't watching a game. That's just what they told us. They're doing secret stuff, and we're going to find out what."

"I already know," Helen said. "That's why you're here. You can't miss this. It's priceless."

"Where did that fried chicken come from?" Caroline said. "Josh isn't supposed to be eating fried anything. He's got to get in shape for his tour."

She felt a tug on the back of her dress. "Sit down," Helen hissed. "Worry about the chicken later."

As they peeked through the ornamental trees, the men trailed into the conservatory and sat on the well-padded sofas. Mitch, Josh's best friend and the only single man among them, put a six-pack on the coffee table before sitting.

"Right." Andrew McInnes, Helen's husband and Josh's father, looked around the group. "Have you all got your books with you?"

"Books?" Jena whispered, her eyes wide.

"Sh," Caroline hissed.

Mitch, Josh, Flynn, and Matt all held up their phones, while Andrew held up a paperback.

"You're reading on your phones?" Andrew said in disgust.

"It's the only way to make sure the wife doesn't know what I'm reading," Flynn said.

"Or that you *can* read," his cousin Matt grinned at him.

"That too, dickhead." Flynn threw a cushion at Matt. "Remind me, why are you here again?"

"Someone's got to keep you out of trouble. I'm pretty sure that's the same reason Mitch is here. As Josh's keeper."

"I don't need a keeper," Josh said, and everyone burst out laughing. He rolled his eyes at them. "Can we get on with this? The kids could get back up at any minute."

"Katy will settle everybody down again," Flynn said with confidence.

"Katy's five," Josh said.

"And already a genius," Flynn said.

"The kids will be fine," Andrew said. "We're no' here to

talk about them. We're here to talk about the book. Now, have you all read it?"

They nodded.

"Good," Andrew said. "What did you think?"

"I had a problem with the hero," Mitch said. "He turned into a cat. That's deeply disturbing. Did anyone else worry about that?"

"I had a look online," Matt said. "There are millions of these shifter books."

"Do you think it's a bestiality thing?" Flynn said. "Because I work with animals, and that's seriously, disturbingly wrong."

"They don't have sex with the men while they're in animal form," Andrew said. "Mainly, they just pat them when they're cats. I think it's a comfort thing. I think this author is trying to tell us that women want to snuggle."

"With someone furry," Josh said. "I don't do furry."

"You don't have to be furry." His dad scowled at him. "If you're worried about the soft, furry part, get one of those fuzzy blankets and wrap Caroline in that before you snuggle."

There was a choking noise from beside Caroline.

Abby grinned wide at her. "I take it back," she whispered. "This is the best girls' night out ever."

"I want to talk about what they did on page one hundred and twenty-seven," Matt said. "I tried that with Jena, and she punched me."

Jena gasped, and Caroline quickly smacked a hand over her mouth. She tugged it away, her eyes wide. "So, *that's* where he got that idea," she whispered.

"Aye," Andrew said, in the tone a college lecturer would use with his first-year students. "That's an advanced technique. I've read hundreds of these romance books now, and I can tell you for a fact that it's better to start off with some of the easier stuff. You don't want to freak your woman out. Especially in bed."

"Are we supposed to bite?" Josh said. "Do women really want us to mark them like that? Or is that just a cat thing? Where does the fiction story stuff end and the female fantasy part begin?"

"That's a good question." Andrew leaned back in his seat and tented his fingers in front of him. "Thoughts?"

"I think it's all real," Mitch said. "I think women like marks of ownership. Why else would they want wedding rings?"

"Exactly." Andrew stopped just short of patting Mitch on the head.

"Women want rings," Matt said, "so they have the gold to sell once they get rid of the guy that came with it."

"Wow, cynical, cuz," Flynn said.

"No," Jena whispered. "Matt's right. I'm totally stocking a war chest in case things go pear-shaped with him."

"With your history, I'm not surprised," Abby said.

"Matt thinks it's cute. He adds to the chest for me." She sighed dreamily. "What kind of man would help you save for the day you might need to leave him?"

"You're both nuts," Abby said. "You know that, right?"

"Yeah." Jena beamed.

"I'm not sure about the biting thing," Josh said, drawing their attention back to the men. "If I bit Caroline, she'd bite back."

"No kidding," Caroline muttered.

"It's sensual biting," Mitch said with a roll of his eyes. "You make it sound like you'd walk into the room, say hi, honey, and then take a chunk out of her neck."

"He's still not biting me," Caroline whispered.

"Which brings me to the vampire in the book," Flynn said. "Anyone else think drinking blood is sexy? Because that just made me want to puke."

The men shuddered.

"I don't know why women think vampires are sexy," Andrew said. "Maybe it's the dark, mysterious, bad-boy thing."

"It's the penetration," Josh said.

The men stared blankly at him.

"Fangs *into* neck. Penetration. It has sexy connotations. I talked to David Boreanaz about this once. Met him at a party, and he said that's why chicks dig vampires. He should know, he made his name playing one."

"Josh is team *Angel* all the way," Mitch said with a smirk.

"Do we even want to know what that means?" Matt said.

"We're getting off topic," Andrew barked. "Focus. Who cares why women find vampires sexy? And the shifter thing has nothing to do with how weirdly attached they are to cats. These books are all about the female fantasy, and that's what we need to tap into." He waved his book. "They've literally written a manual on relationships; all we need to do is decipher the code. Shifters means they want to snuggle. Vampires means they like a little danger with their snuggling. It's that simple."

"Now that I think about it, what's with all this 'mine' stuff?" Flynn said. "Every second page, the guy's grabbing the girl and growling *mine*. And now that I think about it, what's with the growling? When was the last time you growled anything? Other than a growl. Seriously, try it. Can you growl a word?"

"I can burb the alphabet," Josh said.

"Sexy," Mitch drawled.

Caroline wiped her eyes as she slumped against her mother-in-law. Her diaphragm hurt from holding in her laughter. On her other side, Jena had her face pressed into her handbag to muffle her laughter. Abby held her belly with one hand, her other hand over her mouth as she silently laughed —the tears streaming down her face. There was a good chance they'd all pass out before the book club meeting was over.

"Seriously, dude, I can do it. It's like my secret skill." And then Josh proceeded to burb the alphabet.

By the time he reached H, the women were laughing so hard they could barely stay upright. And it was becoming harder to muffle the sound.

"Can you hear something?" Matt asked.

"Oh no." Abby sucked in a breath.

"Just stay still and very quiet," Caroline whispered.

"No. I mean, oh no, my water just broke."

All eyes turned to her.

"It was the laughing, I think," she said.

Jena's head snapped back. "Matt! Flynn! We're having babies out here!"

Helen smacked her on the back of the head. "You couldn't wait until we made it to the front door. Now they'll know we were listening."

The conservatory door crashed open, and the men ran out.

"What the hell?" Josh said when he rounded the plants.

"Hi, honey, we're home a bit earlier than I'd planned," Caroline said.

Abby pointed to the puddle beneath her feet. "I need to go to the hospital," she told Flynn.

Without even flinching at the weight, Flynn swept his wife up into his arms. "Matt, you're driving." He stalked toward Matt's cop car. "Use the sirens. Josh, watch Katy for us. We're having our babies."

Abby snuggled against her husband's chest. "I love you, Flynn Boyle," she said.

"Mine," he told her before kissing her head.

The Breakfast Club

"I feel so used," Mitch told his friends at their weekly breakfast club meeting at the pub.

Lake Benson, owner of Benson Security, cocked an eyebrow at him as his lip twitched. In Lake speak, he was laughing at Mitch. Josh wasn't that subtle, he was laughing so hard he choked on a mouthful of food, and Matt Donaldson, Invertary's entire police force, had to smack him on the back.

Flynn Boyle, ex-footballer and current veterinary student, rushed over to them. He pulled up a chair and sat at their table. "What'd I miss?"

"Jodie's still using Mitch for sex, and he isn't happy about it," Matt told his cousin.

Flynn gaped at Matt. "I ran over here for that? You said *emergency* breakfast club meeting. Having no-strings sex isn't an emergency. It's a gift from the gods."

"Dude," Josh said in disgust. "You told him it was an emergency?"

Matt shrugged and reached for the coffee. "As soon as he answered the phone, he started whining about baby spit. The choice was between telling him to get his backside in gear for an emergency meeting or arrange testosterone injections to cure his hormonal mood swings."

"Dickhead." Flynn shot his cousin the finger.

"The spit-up phase doesn't last," Josh said with the air of authority that came from being father to a toddler. "Once the twins are on solids, it'll get better."

"No more," Mitch pleaded. "Does this look like a mother and baby group? Keep that crap to yourself. We're men. Men don't talk about baby spit."

"I'm with you," Matt said. "I feel like I'm trapped in Baby Land and I don't speak the language. Caroline's pregnant with baby number two, Abby's had twins, Claire's pregnant with her own set of twins. Hell, even Jena's talking about starting a family."

The men froze. Food hovering mid-air on forks.

"Is that a good idea?" Josh voiced what everyone else was thinking. "She can't keep herself in one piece, how will she take care of a kid?"

Matt shook his head in disgust, well aware he was married to the most accident-prone woman in Scotland. A woman who also happened to be a DIY addict. There was a betting pool going in the pub over which power tool she'd use to cause the most damage. So far, the lead bet was on her taking out Matt with a nail gun.

"I said that to her," Matt said, "and she ranted about my 'lack of sensitivity' for half an hour, then kicked me out of the bedroom for the night. Didn't talk to me for a week after it."

Josh let out a whistle. "Talk about overreacting."

"Tell me about it." The cop reached for his coffee.

"You might as well give in," Flynn said. "There's no point arguing. She's going to get what she wants, anyway. Maybe by the time the kid's here, you'll have figured out a way to keep her and the baby alive."

"Bubble wrap!" Josh slammed down his mug. "I'll get

Caroline to do some research, but there must be safety clothes for kids. Something like bubble wrap. At least that way, if she drops the baby, it'll just bounce."

Matt looked grim. "Aye, but that won't stop her walking into a hole with the baby or setting fire to the house while it naps."

"Life was so much easier when all we did with the women in our lives was bed them and run," Flynn said wistfully. "Now they're out of control."

"Speaking of control," Josh said. "Let's get back to the reason for this week's meeting—Mitch has lost what little control he had over his craptastic relationship with Jodie. She only wants to use him as a sex toy, while he wants more. He doesn't know how to address this situation in order to get what he wants." He waved his arms as though conducting an orchestra. "Discuss."

Mitch glared at his friend, silently promising retribution in his future. Josh looked unfazed. He forked a mouthful of bacon and smiled smugly while he chewed. Casually, Mitch reached for his phone, sneaked a photo of Josh with his fried breakfast, and sent it to Caroline with the caption: *Josh eating bacon.*

"Is this a joke?" Flynn was affronted. "We can talk about Mitch's unrequited love, but we can't talk about baby spit?"

"Get over the baby spit, already. This is serious," Josh said around a mouthful of food that was going to get his ass kicked when his wife checked her phone. "Mitch here needs suggestions for what to do with Jodie. Who's got one? Anybody? Seriously, don't be shy. Any suggestion, no matter how dumb, is better than the nothing he's working with right now."

"Thanks," Mitch said drolly as he pushed away his half-full plate. Suddenly, fried black pudding and sausage didn't look so appetizing.

"Anything for you, brother." Josh thumped his fist over his heart.

"Just move in with her." Flynn tugged Mitch's plate toward him and proceeded to polish off the leftovers. "That's what I did. Abby didn't even notice it'd happened until it was too late."

"Can't. Even if I could sneak it past Jodie, her brother would notice. Deke can't keep his nose out of anything."

"Pity she's English. Otherwise, you could marry her to keep her in the country," Matt mused. "That worked for me."

"What about a business arrangement?" Josh pointed a loaded fork at him. "I hooked Caroline with one."

"No you didn't. I was there, remember? She married you to get her hands on the castle."

"That's how it started, but in the end she couldn't resist my charms. That woman is gone for me." He huffed on his nails then buffed them on his *Breakfast Club* T-shirt.

"What charms?" Matt said. "The whole town is still trying to figure out what she sees in you."

"He can sing," Flynn offered helpfully.

"I'm not sure that's enough to put up with him," Matt said.

"Good point," Flynn agreed.

"This is pointless." The whole conversation was just making Mitch feel more hopeless. "Jodie doesn't want a relationship, business or otherwise. Every time I broach the subject, she shuts it down and gets a look in her eyes that says she's about to run for the hills." He sounded pathetic. Any minute now he'd be dyeing his hair black and writing emo poetry.

"Are you sure *you* want a relationship?" Flynn speared a sausage from his cousin's plate, earning himself a glare. "Or is it just that Jodie's the first woman who doesn't come running when you snap your fingers? I mean, you spent years telling us how you're good with being single. Seems a little suspect that you suddenly want Jodie. Maybe the fact she doesn't want you is what's attracting you. The interest will fade once you catch her. You sure you want that to happen?"

"Have you been reading Abby's *Cosmo* again?" Mitch asked and received the same one fingered salute he'd shared with his cousin.

"It was the stabbing," Josh said. "It changed his life, and he realized he didn't want to die old and alone. He had an epiphany."

Matt snorted. "He didn't have an epiphany. He had morphine. A man doesn't decide he wants a relationship just because he gets stabbed."

As usual, they were getting off track. Mitch held up a hand to get their attention. "Even though Dr. Phil over there thinks my relationship is some form of PTSD—"

"Dude," Josh interrupted. "You don't have a relationship. You have booty calls. That's why we're here."

"—I just want more of a commitment from Jodie than hit-and-run sex."

"Can't we Google the answer to wooing Jodie?" Matt said. "There's got to be a site somewhere that lists ways to romance a woman. I'm sure all you need to do is buy her some flowers and chocolate then declare undying love. Women love that crap."

If only it were that simple. "Romantic gestures won't work. Jodie hates them."

"Women say that, but they don't mean it," Flynn said. "It's a trap."

"You're all idiots," Lake said, and he wasn't wrong. "Mitch can't do what you guys did. It wouldn't work for him. He needs to go with his strengths. He needs to formulate a plan of attack and treat this like another business deal he's putting together. He's known for his sharp negotiation skills and for getting what he wants. Do the same with Jodie. Research. Plan. Execute. That's the way to go. Preparation wins the war."

The men stared at him for a few minutes, dumbstruck by the volume of words that had just come out of his mouth.

"How many sentences was that?" Josh looked around at the others. "Ten? Twelve? I think that's a new record."

Grunt, or Samuel Dayton to those who took their lives into their own hands by using his given name, strode up to the table. The American was built like a tank, used even fewer syllables than Lake and was wrapped around the finger of Matt's younger sister Claire.

He slapped a folder down in front of Mitch.

"What's that?" Josh reached for it, but Mitch smacked his hand away.

"It's a background report on Jodie. I need all the help I can get."

"As a cop," Matt said. "I'd like to point out that you are seriously skirting the stalker laws."

"As a lawyer," Mitch said. "I'd like to point out that I have a degree in skirting the law."

With a shrug that said he'd tried, Matt turned to his brother-in-law. "You staying for breakfast?"

"Claire's pregnant," was Grunt's reply.

"Claire's been pregnant for weeks," Flynn said. "She'll be pregnant for a whole lot longer before the babies pop out. You've got time to eat."

"Priorities," Grunt said. "Got to look out for my wife." With that, he turned and stalked back out the door.

"I seriously worry about him." Flynn watched the big guy go.

"You know," Josh said as Mitch flicked through the folder, looking for an angle to use to get through to Jodie. "You're missing one obvious play here."

"What's that, oh wise one?" Mitch didn't look up from his reading.

"You have an agreement with Jodie," Josh said. "Friends with benefits, right?"

"So?" Mitch said.

"So," Josh said. "Seems like she's only keeping half the deal. You need to enforce the other half. How can you be friends with benefits if you don't have the 'friends' part? And what is dating but a form of friends with benefits? Just tell her you want to be friends, then hang out, get to know her and worm your way in when she isn't looking."

Four men stared at Josh with open mouths.

"What?" Josh shrugged. "I have a brain."

"Said the scarecrow," Flynn muttered before turning to Mitch. "The guy who makes a living singing love songs has a point."

"Could it be that simple?" Mitch felt his heart lurch at the thought. "I just make her spend more time with me? I invoke the friends' clause?"

"Right now, what you've got," Josh said, "is a booty call arrangement. It isn't friends with benefits. You need to up the friends part. And what happens when a woman becomes friends with a guy?" There was silence. Josh looked at them like they were idiots. "Emotional attachment. They become attached. The physical stuff becomes confused with the friend stuff and the next thing they know, they're falling in love. They can't help themselves. It's in their DNA."

"I hate to say it," Matt said, "but he makes sense. You need to invoke the friends' clause."

"Did Josh just come up with a plan?" Flynn said.

The rest of the men stared at Josh, who was grinning widely. "I am the *man*." He puffed out his chest—just as Caroline stalked into the bar.

"Josh McInnes, what did we agree about fried food?" She aimed straight for her husband.

And Josh's eyes flew to Mitch. "Asshole. You sold me out."

Mitch didn't even bother to deny it. He just grinned and settled in to watch the fireworks while he plotted how to rope Jodie into a friendship with a man who wanted so much more.

The Reverend Morrison's Last Christmas in Invertary

THIS STORY TAKES PLACE AFTER CALLUM AND
ISOBEL GET MARRIED, WHICH HAPPENS
BETWEEN RAGE AND RANSOM.

During his forty-seven-year tenure at Invertary's Pres-byterian church in the Scottish Highlands, Reverend Morrison had seen it all. And most of it he wished he hadn't. Which was why, on his eightieth birthday, he'd decided to retire to Spain and spend his last few years in a country that wasn't wet and freezing for eleven months of the year.

He'd planned his escape right down to the last detail and made it clear to all and sundry that he didn't want any farewell parties, he just wanted to leave. It had been his intention to give his last sermon at the Christmas morning service—mainly because that was an easy one to prepare—then slip away quietly at the end. As usual, the folk of Invertary completely ignored him. Which is how he found himself taken hostage by his congregation and forced to sit through the longest goodbye since the von Trapp family escaped Austria.

"Reverend Morrison," Caroline McInnes said when she took over his service. "We know you wanted to sneak away, but we couldn't let your many years of service to this church and community go unmarked. Please, take a seat. We have a few things we'd like to say to you, and then we've put on a wonderful buffet lunch for everyone afterward as a thank you."

"Do you know what would have been a proper thank you?" Morrison said as the singing fool Caroline had married dragged a huge, throne-like chair into the middle of his platform. "If you'd listened to what I told you and let me leave in peace."

"We all know you didn't mean that." Caroline smiled at him.

"Aye," his nemesis piped up from the front row, "I told her how you'd secretly confided in me that you were hoping the church would make a fuss."

Betty McLeod gave him a toothless grin. He'd told her no such thing. This was just another attempt at payback for all the years he'd rebuffed her advances. Bloody demon of a woman. If Saint Peter had been around at the same time as Betty, he'd have performed an exorcism on her.

"I did not say that," he told Caroline as she took his arm and led him to the chair.

"I know." She patted his shoulder and then proceeded to ignore him. "Now, since you're heading off to Spain, the children have prepared an appropriate Christmas song for you."

The kids were still dressed in the costumes for the nativity play they'd put on during the service. One of the wise men was picking his nose and wiping it on his crown, while it looked like an angel had spilled orange juice down the front of her white robes—at least, he hoped it was juice, and not vomit stains.

"You." He pointed at a teenager in the front row. "Go to the office and get my angina medicine. I'm going to need it." When the teen didn't move, he barked, "Now!" That got him running.

Morrison was jealous. There was a day, long ago, when he would have sprinted out of the church after the teen. As it was, he was too old and stiff to make a run for it, so all he could do was endure the kids' tuneless rendition of 'Feliz Navidad.' Some fool had given them castanets to play during it. They clicked them randomly and used them to snap at each other. And then, halfway through the song, Mary Johnson—who believed every service should have some dancing in the aisle, and had the biblical evidence to prove it —appeared beside the children. Dressed in Spanish national costume, she performed the Flamenco to the last verse of the song.

It was hell.

It didn't help that Josh McInnes and his breakfast club buddies were sitting right in his line of sight, laughing so hard they had to hold each other up. That's when Morrison real-ized Josh was as much behind his torture as Betty. It was payback for those marriage lessons he'd made him sit through years earlier.

"Well, wasn't that wonderful?" Caroline said as the singing ended. "Let's give them a round of applause."

That's when the scream went up.

"James is peeing!" wailed the back half of the donkey as the front half lost control of his bladder. Parents ran and the donkey, both halves, was whisked away to the toilets.

"Moving along," Caroline said. "The women of Knit or Die have something they'd like to give you." She motioned to Margaret, the leader of the subversive knitting group that had once yarn bombed his pulpit in protest over having to sing the new tune to 'Amazing Grace' instead of the old one that they were used to.

"Great," Morrison muttered. "Just what I need. Woolen crap for a country where the sun always shines."

He stared out of the side window, watching the gray sky as

snow fell softly to cover the town. Bloody Scottish winters. They were the bane of his arthritis.

"Reverend," Margaret said as she stood on the platform, flanked by her cronies. "We realize that you don't have much need for blankets and such in Spain, so we made you a wall hanging. Please accept it with our gratitude."

He tried to get out of the damn chair, but his legs were a tad too short and the seat of the chair too deep. All he could do was rock back and forth, getting nowhere.

"There's no need for the reverend to get up," Caroline said. "But before you give it to him, why don't you hold it up for all of us to see?"

"Oh, aye, good idea." Margaret and Shona unfolded the hanging and held it up.

It looked like a Sunday school craft project in wool. Just what he wanted to take all the way to Spain.

"As you can see," Margaret said. "We've knitted scenes from the town." She pointed at the top. "These are the hills, with the old mine. This is the High Street and the church. That's the Scottie Dog pub, and that's the loch."

"And," Jean said, stepping forward with a large plastic bag. "We also knitted everyone in town and added Velcro to their backs so you can place them wherever you want." She rummaged in the bag and came out with a short, grumpy-faced man, dressed in black with a white dog collar. No prizes for guessing who that was.

"Look." She stuck the knitted version of him to the front of the church and then beamed at him as though she'd done something miraculous.

The congregation must have thought so too because there was applause.

"But wait," Shona said. "There's more."

Oh God, please, no more, he begged, but clearly, God wasn't inclined to give him relief.

"I made you this." Shona held up what appeared to be a lime green knitted bag with long straps. Maybe a plant holder? "It's a mankini," Shona said, as though reading his mind, or possibly the confusion on his face. "Like a bikini, only for men. You put your...privates...in the pouch and the straps go over your shoulders. It's for wearing on the beach."

"That looks wonderful," Caroline said with a smile that was clearly forced. "And you chose a pattern that offered plenty of ventilation, which is good, seeing as Spain is so hot. Why don't you put it all in the bag and we'll move on to the next item? We don't want the food getting cold."

The women did just that, patting his hands and hugging him before returning to their seats.

"I'd like everyone who has been baptized by Reverend Morrison to stand up," Caroline said, and a good half of the packed church stood. "Now I'd like everyone who's been married by him to stand." More people joined the first group. "Now anyone who's had him perform the funeral of a loved one." Yet more people got to their feet.

Caroline turned to him. "Look around you," she said. "How many people can say they've touched so many lives in one lifetime? And these are just the ones who could be here today." She pointed at Dougal, who stood holding a microphone in the center aisle.

The pub owner was wearing a red shirt with an ivy pattern on it and a shiny green waistcoat over the top. With his white beard, he looked like Santa had raided Elton John's wardrobe for the morning. "Reverend," he boomed, making Morrison wonder why anyone had given him a mic. "You performed both my marriage ceremonies, laid my dear departed wife to rest and faithfully visited my mother in the hospital until she passed away. You've also propped up my bar on occasion, offered unwanted advice to anyone who would listen, and you're a terrible dominoes player, isn't he boys?" The Domino Boys cheered. "You will be greatly missed."

He passed the mic to Matt Donaldson, the town's police force. "You performed my dad's funeral, married me off to the woman of my dreams after letting her claim asylum in your church." He smiled down at his wife Jena, who had her arm in a cast after her latest DIY disaster. "And you made time to talk to each of us regularly after dad passed away, just to make sure, as you put it, that we weren't suicidal or fighting the urge to turn to drink." He grinned. "You will be greatly missed."

He passed the mic to Kirsty Benson. The ex-model and current underwear designer beamed at him, and he felt his heart melt a little. He'd always had a soft spot for Kirsty. "You were at my christening, you sat through all my terrible Sunday school plays, you were there to comfort us when my dad died, and you came to Spain to visit me in hospital after the car accident that ended my career. All of this was done with your usual bad cheer, but you did it with love. You will be greatly missed."

Morrison cleared his throat and fidgeted in his chair. Beside him, the lights on the Christmas tree flickered as the vast church seemed to grow smaller. He wanted to shout out that they could stop now, that this wasn't needed; he hadn't gone into the ministry seeking recognition or thanks. But there was no stopping them now. The microphone passed from person to person, each one finishing their list of memories with "You will be greatly missed."

Until Betty McLeod got her hands on the mic.

"Okay, you old bas—" Betty started, but Lake Benson, who was standing beside her, smacked a hand over her mouth.

"This is a church," he said. "You're already going to hell, try not to take the rest of us with you."

She glared up at him as she shoved his hand away. "As I was saying before I was so rudely interrupted by the morality police, Reverend Morrison, you old *basket case* you." She gave Lake a smug look that said she thought she was smarter than him. But then, Betty thought she was smarter than everybody. "*Morry*, you've been a pain in my arse for decades. Just when I had things how I liked, you'd turn up and tell everybody it's morally wrong, or illegal, or some other such nonsense. Unlike the rest of the idiots in here, I won't greatly miss you. I will miss our games of hide-the-salami though. I enjoyed having a toy boy."

That was it! He launched himself out of the chair that had a death grip on his backside and stalked across the platform to snatch the microphone out of Caroline's hand.

He pointed at Betty. "I did not have sexual relations with that woman."

"Oh, dude, no," Josh McInnes groaned as he climbed onto the platform. "This is not the time to invoke Clinton."

"And another thing," Betty shouted with glee, still holding her mic. "His first name is Shirley." There was a gasp, followed by smothered sniggers. "That's right," Betty said. "His full name is Shirley Thomas Morrison," she paused, "the second!" And then she burst into a witch's cackle.

"Give me that." Lake pried the mic from her hands. "Sorry Rev," he said before switching it off and tossing it to Josh.

"Okay, everybody, calm down," Josh said, flashing that famous smile of his that seemed to turn smart women into fools. "We all know that the Rev hasn't had sex with Betty."

"Yes." Caroline took the mic out of the Reverend's hands and led him back to the chair of doom, while he kept his scowling eyes on Betty. "Because he's a man of the cloth and they don't do that."

"Or," Josh said, "because he has enough sense to keep

away from Gollum over there." He grinned at the crowd. "See what I did there? Lake calls her his Hobbit, but really, she's the corrupted version of those lovable shire creatures. Evil has turned her into Gollum. Smart, eh?"

There were groans. Caroline shook her head and stepped in front of her husband. "Josh is now going to stop talking, and start singing."

There was a cheer. Morrison suspected it was more for Josh shutting up than for his singing. He looked at the American. "If this is 'White Christmas,' I will make it my duty to pray daily that you lose your voice mid-concert."

Josh just grinned as the music started and he launched into a rendition of 'Hit the Road Jack.' Smart arse. Although, it did bring a smile to his face when they got to the part about the meanest old woman he'd ever seen, and the church sang it to Betty. It would have been perfect if she hadn't taken a bow and cackled as though they were giving her adulation. Oh, but he couldn't wait to get away from that woman.

There was loud applause when Josh finished singing. Morrison signaled to one of the kids to bring him his cane. He was getting out of there before he got trapped during lunch and led down the long road of reminiscing.

"Oh, we're not finished yet," Caroline said, making him groan as he sat back in his chair. "The children have prepared one last special song for you."

As they rushed onto the stage and the first bars of music played, Reverend Morrison knew that this was God's retribution for being the world's most surly minister. Because the children were singing, 'So Long, Farewell,' from *The Sound of Music.*

Betty Wants Grandkids

THIS STORY HAPPENS BETWEEN RELENTLESS
AND RAGE, AFTER CAUGHT IN THE INVERTARY
BOOKS.

B etty McLeod pushed open the door to the Eye Spy security shop and stomped inside.

"Outta ma way!" She swung her handbag at Lake Benson's newest recruit, hitting him in the stomach.

"Oof." The wimp rubbed his belly and glared down at her.

Betty just smirked at him. It would be a cold day in hell before she was intimidated by an oversized pup. Lake was hiring his security team members younger and younger these days. This one used to be a cop. Betty narrowed her eyes at him. She couldn't see it. He barely looked old enough to shave.

She stalked to her La-Z-Boy and plopped into it. Wiggling until she got her bum in just the right dent to make it comfortable.

"You want to stop hitting my team?" Lake said from behind the counter.

"No." Betty scowled at the man she considered her son. "They're in the way. Can't you send them out on a job? Somewhere dangerous."

Lake's lip twitched, which for him was equivalent to

showing full-blown hysteria. Now *he* didn't look like a boy. He looked like a proper man, capable of taking care of any situation he came across. There was a touch of gray coming in around the temple area of his blond hair, but apart from that, he looked just as fierce and handsome as when she'd first met him. Some people found the ex-SAS specialist intimidating. Not Betty. She considered Lake to be her equal—someone brave enough to stand up to her. Not that he ever won, mind you.

"Get me a cup of tea, *princess*," she ordered the newbie.

Max's jaw clenched as he stared at Lake. "I swear, one of these days, I will kill her and bury the body where no one can find it."

"Get in line," Lake said with a snort.

"Am I getting my tea?" Betty snapped. "I'm not getting any younger here."

"Astrid," Lake called into the back room, "bring Satan a cup of tea. Double the arsenic this time."

There was a giggle. Astrid was another spineless addition to Benson Security. "When are you going to hire some grown-ups?" Betty said. "Our team is meant to be scary. This lot couldn't intimidate a flea. I mean, look at him." She pointed at the new guy, Max. "Get. A. Haircut."

"Lake..." The man-child clenched and unclenched his fists, making Betty cackle.

"See what I mean?" Betty pointed at Max. "If that's supposed to scare me, then he's wasting his time. Are you sure he was in the police? Was it the real police force, or those guys in ill-fitting uniforms that patrol shopping centers?"

"I'm going to..." Max took a step toward her.

Betty was unimpressed. She dismissed him with a roll of her eyes before raking around in her handbag.

"Max," Lake said. "Go take a break."

"Aye," Betty said as she brought out a brown paper bag with a steaming hot Scotch pie inside. "Away and powder your nose."

He let out a strangled growl and slammed the front door behind him when he left.

"Quit winding up the staff," Lake ordered.

"Quit hiring namby-pamby wee bairns." She took a bite of her pie. "Where's my tea?" she said around a mouthful of food, almost losing her false teeth in the process.

A piece of crust fell out her mouth and onto her favorite tartan dress. She picked it up and popped it back in. When she looked up, Lake was shaking his head at her.

"What?" she demanded.

"I swear you get worse every year."

"Thanks." She gave him a grin.

There was a noise behind Lake, and a tall, gangly brunette came through carrying a tray with a teapot, a cup and a plate of biscuits. Betty sniffed. Okay, so maybe not all the new recruits were totally useless.

The girl put the tray on the table beside Betty's old chair, which sat in the corner of the shop. She scurried away, without even looking Betty in the eye.

"I thought you said this one had more backbone than the last receptionist?" Although to be fair, at least Betty saw Astrid now and then; she'd only ever spotted Julia from a distance.

"She's perfectly fine around *normal* people," Lake said.

Betty took his dig as a compliment. She'd never aspired to normalcy.

"You know, it's sexist to hire women for reception and men as security specialists." She took another bite of her pie.

"I have women on my security team."

"Aye, Megan Donaldson." Betty shook her head in disgust. "I don't see why you made her a trainee but wouldn't make me one. Her only experience is dyeing the Baxter sheep pink. I have a lot more tricks than that up my sleeve."

Lake stopped going over the paperwork in front of him. "You're eighty-nine. You're too old to be a trainee."

"I'm still fit." She sat up straighter as though that would prove it.

"A snail can run faster than you."

"But can it outthink me?" She tapped her temple.

Lake huffed a laugh. "I'm not taking you on as a trainee. You're a liability just hanging out in the shop."

"Coward. I'm going to call Callum and make him give me a job in London. He's got more spine than you *and* a better attitude. He's my favorite now."

"I'll make sure to give him a call and congratulate him."

Betty narrowed her eyes at him. "At least he's Scottish."

Lake pointed to his face. "Look how little I care," he said in that poncey English accent of his.

Betty had just opened her mouth to tell him where to stick his amused face, when the door opened and Lake's wife, Kirsty, walked in. She spotted Betty and her shoulders slumped, brightening Betty's day no end.

"Great, *you're* here," Kirsty said to Betty before rounding the counter to give Lake a kiss.

"This is my chair," Betty said. It'd been her chair for years. Ever since she'd owned the town's only underwear shop. She'd commanded an empire from that chair. "Where else would I be?"

"I thought you'd joined the Domino Boys. I thought you were playing dominoes at the pub." Kirsty leaned into Lake, her long red hair curling about her face and around the scars on her neck—a reminder of the car accident, years earlier, that had ended her modeling career.

"I did." Betty tugged at her hairnet to straighten it before reaching for her tea. "But they were boring. All they talk about is their ailments. If I wanted to listen to that crap, I'd hang out at the doctor's surgery. What happened to real men? The ones who'd lose a limb, grit their teeth and get on with it? Like our new London boss. Callum lost his legs, but do you hear him whine about it? No. Whereas other men whine like two-year-olds when they stub their bloody toes. I blame the estrogen. They've added it to the water. Now men cry at the least wee thing, and then they grow boobs." She eyed Lake's chest thoughtfully. "You look okay, but I'd keep an eye on it."

"You're talking rubbish again. Nobody's added estrogen to the water," Kirsty said before shaking her head and turning to Lake. "I need to talk to you. In private."

"Don't worry," Betty said. "You can talk here. My lips are sealed."

They both looked at her like there were soap bubbles coming out of her mouth.

Kirsty's lips thinned. "We're not talking about our private business in front of you, so you can get that thought right out of your head."

"Why not? I know everything anyway." Honestly, she was beginning to think Kirsty was losing IQ points as she got older. Betty remembered her as being much smarter as a child. Hell, back then she'd at least had the good sense to run when she saw Betty coming.

Kirsty looked up at Lake. "Let's go upstairs to your office."

He ran a hand down his wife's hair, and his face softened. "Okay."

"Look," Betty said. "If this is about you not being able to have bairns, I already know."

Kirsty gasped, and Lake's face hardened.

"What?" Betty held up her hands. "Was it a secret? I don't see what all the fuss is about. So you can't have babies. Neither could I, and everything turned out fine for me."

"Betty," Lake rumbled in the tone he used to intimidate the minions.

She snorted her amusement. It was sweet when he thought that would work on her. She dug into her handbag and brought out some papers she'd printed off from her new computer.

"Back in my day," she said, "we didn't have the interweb. Now you can get anything on there. Even kids. I had a look for you and circled the ones I like." She thrust out an arm, papers in hand, shaking it when nobody took them.

With a tight frown, Lake leaned over the counter and took the papers. He smoothed them out in front of him while Kirsty continued to gape at her.

"How do you know about the...the..." The color drained from her face.

"About the injuries from the accident meaning you can't have babies?" Betty tapped her nose. "I have my sources. That's why Lake should hire me as a trainee."

"But...but..." Kirsty looked up at Lake as she turned even whiter.

"Don't faint," Lake ordered, like that would stop it happening. He reached behind him, pulled up a stool, and lifted Kirsty onto it. "Astrid? Water!"

A couple of seconds later, the new receptionist scurried through with a bottle of water, took one look at their faces, and ran away again.

"No backbone," Betty said in disgust.

"How do you know about Kirsty's situation?" Lake's deadly tone would have made anyone else pee their pants. Not Betty. Mainly it just made her beam with pride.

"That doesn't matter." She waved a dismissive hand. "The point is, you two need to stop feeling sorry for yourselves and give me some grandkids. I'm not getting any younger, and I want to pass on my knowledge before I kick the bucket."

"I think I'm going to be sick," Kirsty said.

"Drama queen," Betty muttered as she wriggled her way out of her chair and stomped over to the counter. She spread out the papers. "I saw on the interweb that you can get babies from all over the world. That actress, Angela Jolly, has one from every continent. You can pick them out with your shopping, and they deliver them. I'm not sure how much they cost. The web people were a bit offended when I asked and wondered if I was an undercover cop or something." She beamed at them. "Must be the security training paying off. Anyway, I'm sure you make enough money to afford a couple." She pulled another piece of paper toward her. "This place will even let you put in an order, and they'll get you exactly what you want."

Kirsty groaned and put her head between her knees.

Betty ignored her. "I already sent them a computer letter asking if they could get us one with red hair and an English accent, just in case you want a kid that's like the two of you."

"I'm going to pass out," Kirsty wailed.

Lake pinched the bridge of his nose and took several deep breaths before looking at Betty. His eyes were ice. Betty cocked her head and considered him. She'd never seen that look before.

"Satan, you've outdone yourself this time." Lake pointed at the website that said they'd provide kids to order. "This is bloody illegal. They're probably kidnapping children. I don't even know how you found this site, but I'll pass it on to my government contacts and get it shut down."

Betty looked at the printout and frowned. "I found it on the hidden interweb."

"You mean the dark web?" Lake's voice sounded tinny. "How the hell did you get onto the dark web?"

"I watched a video. Now that I think about it, the guy who told you how to do it didn't show his face. I thought he was camera shy. I should have guessed he was a criminal. Now, if I'd had Benson Security training, I wouldn't have made that mistake."

Lake's jaw clenched.

Betty ignored him and pointed to a Chinese organization. "What about one of these? This wee lassie looks feisty; I like that. That's if you want a girl. I don't see the problem, girls are smarter, but you might want a boy."

"Please, tell me you realize that adopting a child isn't the same as picking out new curtains?" Kirsty said, still facing the floor.

Betty looked at the printouts, then up at Lake who shook his head to tell her not to answer the question.

"I don't see why you're making a fuss. You wanted kids. I sorted it for you. The least you could do is say thanks." Betty grinned. "And name your daughter after me. Betty Benson. Sounds good, aye?"

With a whistled tune and a spring in her step, Betty left them to think about it. As the door closed behind her, she headed back for the pub and the Domino Boys. She put her hand into her huge bag and pulled out something else she'd found on the interweb. It was a gift for the Domino Boys. She grinned at the knitted plaque that said: *Domino Players Do It With Viagra*. She planned to tell them it was from the Knit or Die women and get Dougal to put it up behind the bar.

With a cackle, she watched the sun sparkle on the loch as she headed down Main Street. Maybe she'd get some fern cakes on the way. It seemed like the perfect day for cake.

"Take a deep breath," Lake said as he crouched in front of his wife.

"That woman is the bane of my life." Kirsty's big blue eyes stared into his soul, and Lake felt his heart melt all over again.

She was perfection. And she was his.

"How did she know about my fertility problems?" Kirsty said.

"I think she's bugged the place," Lake said. "I found discrepancies in the inventory. A couple of listening devices were missing."

"Please." Kirsty put a hand on his cheek. "Please let one of the new team members take her out."

His head fell back, and he roared with laughter. Only Kirsty could make it bubble out of him. He pressed a gentle kiss to her soft, pink lips.

"I can't do that. She'd just come back to haunt us."

"There is that." Kirsty pushed her hair out of her face. "You're going to shut down that disgusting baby operation though, right?"

"Oh yes," Lake promised. Even if he had to do it personally.

"And maybe you should restrict your pet Hobbit's internet access while you're at it," Kirsty said.

Lake figured he had more chance of getting the world to spin in a different direction. "I'll get right on that," he said instead.

Kirsty wasn't fooled, but her eyes sparkled as she wrapped her arms around his neck. "I've got the tickets."

He felt a rush of adrenaline surge through him. "When do we leave?"

"Tonight. Ten o'clock flight out of Glasgow. I've packed

already." Her eyes filled with tears, which she blinked back rapidly. "Can you believe we're going to get our baby?"

"I can't wait." Lake gave her a hard kiss that left them both breathless. When they broke apart, he rested his forehead on hers. "You know Betty will think this was her idea."

Kirsty let out a sigh. "I don't care what she thinks, but we aren't calling our daughter Betty. We can get a dog and name it after her. A Doberman. One that drools."

Lake chuckled. "Come on, let's get out of here and get on the road."

"You're right, we need to get going," Kirsty said as he stood and tugged her to her feet. "It's a long drive to Glasgow."

"It's an even longer flight to China," Lake said.

"I can't wait," Kirsty whispered as they walked out into Invertary's main street.

Aunty Megan Saves the Day

Megan hung up after the call from her mother and promptly sent a text to every member of Benson Security's Scottish office.

Code Green, was all it said.

She raced down the stairs of the house she'd grown up in, grabbed the go-bag she'd stashed in the closet beside the front door when she'd arrived from London, and ran outside. Slamming the door behind her.

"Hey," Dimitri called from where he was clearing out a lifetime's worth of 'man-junk' from her dad's garage. "What's the rush?"

"Code Green," she said as she yanked open the door to their SUV.

Dimitri stopped wrapping the cord around the third sander he'd found, tossed it on the bench and jogged toward her. "I'll drive."

She narrowed her eyes at him. "I'm faster."

"I'm safer."

"We don't need safe. We need fast."

"Did you text your brother?" he asked as he blocked her

from climbing into the car.

"Aye."

"Then we'll have a police escort, and we'll go fast. Fast but safe—so long as you aren't driving. Get your ass in the passenger seat, Buffy. Time's a wasting."

With a huff and a frown, she stomped around the car. "You have one little car crash, and you're branded for life," she muttered.

"One?" Dimitri arched an eyebrow at her, his eyes glittering with amusement.

"Or two," she conceded. Did a crash count if she wasn't the one who'd been injured? "Maybe three, if you count the time we ran Grunt off the road."

"Everybody counts that time." Dimitri put the SUV in gear and headed for the main road out of town.

The sun shone over Invertary, warming the gray stone walls of the houses dotting the hills around the loch. At the bottom of the High Street, the blue waters glistened in the afternoon sun. Home. Even though she now lived in London and traveled all over the world with her job, the tiny Scottish town would always be home to Megan.

"We could always move here," Dimitri said softly. "Transfer to the Scottish office."

She shook her head. "My feet are too itchy for that. I like the international jobs the London office pulls in. Plus, big brother's here, and there's no way he'd let me work as a security specialist without interfering. Then I'd have to kill him, and that would upset Jena."

"Just Jena?" His lips twitched. "Not your mom?"

"Mum's been expecting it for years. It's only a matter of time before Claire or I snap and off him." She cast him a wry look. "You try growing up in a town where your brother's the only cop. Talk about a killjoy." Blue flashing lights up ahead caught her eye. "Speak of the devil."

Dimitri signaled and maneuvered their SUV in behind Matt's police car. And he wasn't the only one. Megan twisted in her seat and spied Lake Benson driving the car behind them, sitting beside him was Joe Barone—her brother-in-law's best friend.

"We're going to need more people," she said.

"Three cars back. Looks like Josh and Mitch."

"What the hell use are a singer and a suit? We need people with guns."

There was silence for a beat. "Please tell me you didn't bring a gun."

Megan didn't answer, because he'd specifically said *not* to tell him.

Dimitri heaved a sigh. "You can't go in armed."

She didn't think that rated an answer either, because she could *definitely* go in armed.

"Give me your backpack," he ordered.

"Not going to happen."

"I'm your superior. You're still a trainee. When I give you an order in the field, you'd damn well better obey."

There was so much wrong with his statement that it took Megan a minute to decide what to deal with first. "Nobody's my superior. We aren't in the field. This isn't a job. And you aren't in charge. So, you can stuff your order right up—"

A car shot past them, and one of Lake's men saluted from the passenger window.

"At last." Megan breathed a sigh of relief. "Some decent backup. I bet nobody's asked them if they have guns."

She couldn't wait until she lost her trainee-badass status and her right to bear arms was no longer under question. Although, that right might only hold up in America. She needed to Google that.

"Whatever you're thinking," Dimitri said. "Stop it."

"Just get us to Fort William and let me deal with the rest."

"We should have rented a house there for the duration," Dimitri said for the millionth time since they'd arrived in Scotland three days earlier.

"Don't you think it's enough that my crazy brother-in-law moved his wife and mother-in-law there two months ago, 'Just to be safe'? Invertary's close enough. We'll get there in plenty of time."

He shot her a skeptical look. "Are you sure? How long does it take to have a baby?"

"Two babies. And it takes as long as it takes." She shuddered at the thought of suffering through days of pain pushing out not one but two human beings. "I'm never having kids. You do know that, right?"

"Buffy." He said in the tone he used when talking her out of her underwear.

"I'm serious. Twins run in our family. You saw how big Claire got toward the end. She looked like she'd swallowed a bus. Her ankles had swollen to the same width as my thighs. And all she did was cry. Nothing on this green earth would make me go through that."

He glanced at her with molten eyes that made her clench her thighs together. "Nothing?"

She swallowed hard, determined to resist the power of his sex appeal. "Nothing. Still want to marry me?" She couldn't help holding her breath as she waited for the answer.

His grin was pure sexual promise. "You don't get out of it that easy."

"Whatever," she said, trying to sound casual as a wave of relief swept through her.

"Speaking of weddings," Dimitri said as they zoomed along the highway. "We've got time to talk before we hit Fort William. How about we set a date for the big day?"

Megan groaned and sank into her seat. "How about the tenth of never? That good for you?"

A look of sheer determination crossed his face. "You ever been to Vegas?"

"The only way you're getting me to Vegas is by drugging me and carrying me onto the plane."

He nodded. "Sounds like a plan."

Megan just shook her head as her phone buzzed in her hand. It was a text from her mother:

S.O.S The beast is loose. I repeat, the beast is loose.

"Better step on it," she said as she rang her brother. "Or there won't be a hospital to visit when we get there."

Dimitri put his foot down while Megan spoke to Matt. "Pick up the pace," she said when he answered. Mum says Grunt has gone full Hulk. This is a full-blown Code Green situation."

Matt muttered something under his breath before raising his voice. "Stay behind me. I'll clear the way." There was a pause. "Please tell me you aren't driving."

Megan hung up on him.

⚜

THEY HEARD GRUNT BEFORE THEY SAW HIM. THE WHOLE hospital shuddered with his roar.

"It's all under control," Matt called as he led their group through the corridors toward the shouting. "Stay back."

In front of Megan, and behind her brother, were Lake and Joe. Dimitri was on one side of her, Josh McInnes on the other. Behind her were Mitch and the rest of Lake's Scottish team. She was surrounded by testosterone—and Josh.

"Remind me why you're here again?" she asked the singer.

"Are you implying I'm useless?" He grinned like that was funny.

Her cousin Flynn, an ex-professional footballer, appeared beside them. "Sorry I'm late to the party. And nobody's *implying* you're useless, we're saying it outright. You need to train, or you're going to die during your next concert tour. Tomorrow morning, you come running with me."

Josh tripped over his own feet, head-butting Joe in the back. "Sorry," he said to Joe. "Run?" he said to Flynn like it was an alien concept. "For fun?"

"No," Flynn said. "For fitness." He eyed Josh, who wore an *Iron Man* T-shirt. "We'll throw in some weights as well."

"Yeah, I'm too busy to run," Josh said. "Got to work on the album."

"I'm sure Caroline could help clear your schedule." Flynn grinned and the men around him chuckled. Josh's wife had been trying for years to get him fitter.

"You're all assholes," Josh grumbled. "Except for you," he told Megan. "You're just scary."

"Thanks," she said as they rounded a corner and screeched to a halt.

Two hospital security guards blocked their path. Several nurses stood in doorways while patients and their families peeked out into the corridor through their windows. Two men in scrubs inched toward Grunt; their hands held out in front of them. Behind them stood another security guard, who looked like he was either about to run or wet himself. And, in the middle of all this, Megan's mountain of a brother-in-law towered over everyone as he held a guy in a white coat against the wall by his throat.

"Grunt." Joe elbowed his way to the front of their group. "What you doing, big guy?"

"Um, going Hulk on the medical staff," Megan said.

"Samuel!" A screech filled the corridor, coming from one of the rooms. Claire wanted her husband.

Grunt's hand tightened on the doctor's throat. If he'd heard Joe, or even registered they were there, it didn't show.

"My wife is in pain," he said to the doctor in a low

growling voice. "You need to stop the pain. My wife doesn't have to deal with pain. *Ever*."

"Oh, this isn't good," Flynn muttered.

"I told you." The doctor clutched Grunt's wrist, holding on as he stretched up on tiptoe. His face, which had turned red, was inching into blue. "It's too late to administer pain relief. We just have to let nature take its course."

"No!" Grunt roared.

"Big guy." Joe stepped forward. "You need to back the hell off. You're damaging Claire's doctor, and she needs him."

Nope. Still didn't penetrate.

"Pain meds," Grunt told the doc.

"Samuel," Claire screamed. "Samuel, I need you."

One of the guys dressed in scrubs stepped toward Grunt. "Listen, Samuel," he said, and everyone who knew Grunt gasped.

"Damn it to hell," Joe snapped. "Julia told everyone in the hospital not to call him that. She sent a memo and everything."

Still holding on to the doctor's throat, Grunt turned his head slowly toward the nurse, who visibly swallowed.

"Big guy." The nurse took another step forward. "Your wife needs you."

"Do not engage," Lake told the man.

Neither Grunt nor the nurse listened.

"Samuel," Claire shouted. "These babies are too big!"

"Samuel." The nurse took another step. "Can I call you Sam?" The idiot smiled while everyone else groaned.

That was when Grunt dropped the doctor, picked up the nurse and tossed him through a window into one of the rooms.

"Everybody, back the hell off," Joe shouted as people screamed.

"Somebody stop Claire's pain," Grunt shouted. "You." He

grabbed the other guy in scrubs. "Make the pain stop."

"Okay. Okay." The guy looked like he was about to pass out. "Let go of me and I'll get some meds."

Megan shook her head in disgust. Even at this distance, you could tell the guy was lying. Grunt tossed him over his shoulder and down the corridor before turning back to the doctor.

En masse, Benson Security descended.

"Grunt, step away from the doctor," Lake ordered.

"Claire's in pain," Grunt shouted, knocking Lake out of his way.

"Arrest him," one of the female nurses called. "Don't just stand there."

"Aye," Matt said. "I'll get right on that."

"Big guy," Joe put a hand on Grunt's arm. "You need to calm the hell down. Claire needs you."

Grunt's fist went back and then connected with Joe's face. And that was the last time Joe spoke for a while. As one, the rest of the men jumped on Grunt, who roared and shook them off like a dog with fleas.

"Dose him," Matt shouted.

"Joe's got the sedative." Lake dodged Grunt's fist.

Mitch dropped to his knees beside the unconscious Joe and searched his pockets. "It's smashed."

"This is a bloody hospital," Flynn snapped as he jumped on Grunt's back. "Somebody get something to knock this guy out."

Grunt threw himself back against the wall, smashing Flynn into it. Flynn let out a strangled whine then slid to the floor.

"This baby's too big," Claire shouted. "Why did I marry a freaking giant? Samuel Dayton get your backside in here and get these monster children out of me." And then she screamed with pain.

Grunt heard the scream and lunged for the doctor, throwing two of Lake's team out of his way. The doctor's face lost all color as he fell to his backside and crab-walked away from the crazy giant.

Megan calmly watched all this from the end of the corridor before reaching into her backpack.

Dimitri saw the move as he tried to get between Grunt and his prey. "You can't shoot him."

Ignoring him, she pulled two fully charged stun guns out of her bag and strode toward Grunt, stepping over Joe and Mitch and dodging everyone else.

"Now I know how the Black Widow feels when she tries to calm the Hulk," she muttered.

Only, she didn't plan on singing him a lullaby.

"Grunt," she snapped, and his head swung toward her.

"Claire?" He seemed confused. And, not for the first time, Megan thanked God that she was an identical twin.

"Samuel," she said, smiling sweetly. "I need you, honey."

His face softened, and he took a step toward her. It was close enough. She shot out both arms and hit him with enough volts to take down Godzilla. His jaw clenched, his face turned red, his arms stiffened, and his eyes rolled back. And then, he toppled to the ground like a felled tree, hitting with a crash that reverberated throughout the building.

Megan stood over him as the men around her wiped blood from their faces and struggled to their feet. All but Joe. He was still out cold.

"Now would be a good time to sedate him," Megan told the doctor. "He gets a bit upset when his wife's in pain."

The doctor gave her a wide-eyed look before nodding and running for the meds room.

Megan looked at her boss. "A syringe? That's what you brought?"

Lake wiped the blood from his mouth with the back of

his hand. "I didn't want to fry his brain."

She looked down at the man-mountain in front of her. "What brain?"

"Samuel," Claire screeched. "Get these unnaturally big-headed babies out of me."

"I'll deal with my sister." Megan stepped over Grunt. "If I were you, I'd cuff him to a chair, and anything else that will keep him down. You can sedate him, but who knows how long that will last."

Lake cocked his head at two of his men, who warily set about cuffing Grunt's hands behind his back.

"These are the last kids these two have," Matt declared. Like he had any say in the matter. Honestly, her brother had a serious God complex.

Megan passed the men and strode into her sister's room. The tension inside was worse than it was outside. Claire lay on the bed, knees up, face red and sweat pouring off her. She had a death grip on their mother's hand, while the midwife checked the machines at the head of the bed.

As soon as Claire spotted Megan, she frowned. "Did you taze him?"

"Had to." Megan strode toward her sister.

"Bloody men," Claire said between pants. "I hate them. All of them. I hate their sperm. And their babies. And sex. I hate sex. I'm never having sex again." Her head spun toward the midwife. "While my husband's out, can you vasectomize him?"

"I don't think that's a good idea, honey," their mother said, looking worried.

At that point, Claire went into full *Exorcist* spinning-head mode. "De-sex that man," she shrieked. And then gasped with pain again.

Megan eyed the midwife. "Just curious, but would it hurt her and the babies if I used my stun gun on her?"

"Megan!" their mother snapped.

"I had to marry a giant," Megan ranted once the contraction passed. "And have giant babies. Not one giant baby. But two. And where is the giant man who caused all this? He's outside being a giant arse to everyone because he can't deal with the pain. It isn't even his pain." She finished on a screech before her hand snapped out and she grabbed the midwife's wrist. "I want a C-section. Now."

As the midwife unpicked Claire's fingers one at a time, there was a scuffle behind them. They turned to watch four men drag an unconscious Grunt into the room, prop him against the wall, and then cuff him to the radiator.

"That's...unusual..." the midwife said.

Just then, the doctor pushed his way past the men filling the room. His face was still red, and it looked like there might be bruising around his throat.

"Everybody out," he snapped, his voice hoarse.

"Did Grunt do that to you?" Claire's eyes were on his throat.

"Let's focus on dealing with these babies before we worry about anything else," the doctor said.

Claire nodded, a manic gleam in her eyes. "Please, could you cut off my husband's balls before he wakes up? It would be payback for both of us, and you'd never have to see him again."

The doctor hesitated before answering, casting a glance at the unconscious Grunt. "Tempting, but how about we deal with you first?"

At that point, Claire hunched over and let out another blood-curdling scream. The doctor went to the foot of her bed and lifted the sheet to peer underneath.

"She's fully dilated; these babies are coming." His voice was filled with relief.

"I think everybody should wait outside now," the midwife

shooed the men out of the room.

"Hi," Josh said. "I'd like to offer you complimentary tickets for my next show, with backstage passes. Just a little something to compensate you for all your trouble."

At the sight of Josh, the woman almost fainted, and a blush stole up her cheeks. "You're Josh McInnes," she gushed. "I love you. I have all your albums."

Josh smiled his award-winning smile at her before shooting Megan a look. "See," he said. "I'm helpful. I smooth the way."

Megan rolled her eyes.

As the room cleared, Dimitri threw an arm around her shoulder. "This could be you one day," he said.

"In your dreams."

"The head's too big," Claire screamed.

"On the plus side," Dimitri said. "We would have normal-sized babies. I don't think they'd hurt this much."

"If you aren't family," the doctor said, "get out."

With that, he flicked back the sheet, and Megan saw more of her sister than she ever wanted to see. And a good chunk of a baby she'd only planned on seeing when it was fully disconnected from its mother.

That's when the room went black, and she hit the floor.

❧

"You're an aunty." Claire cradled a baby, swathed in blue, as she beamed at Megan.

"And you're a mother." Megan still couldn't believe that either of them was old enough to have children, let alone care for them. She looked at her own mother. Didn't you have to be an adult to be a mother? Was she an adult now? Was Claire? Who the hell decided that?

"And I'm a father," Grunt boomed.

The look of wonder on his face almost made up for the carnage he'd caused earlier. He stood beside the bed with a tiny bundle of blue cradled in his arms. His face glowed with awe.

"I have babies," he said. "I'm a father."

"Is he okay?" Megan asked Dimitri. Between the electricity and the drugs, she wasn't sure if there was long-term brain damage.

"Hard to tell," Dimitri said.

"I can't believe we have twins." Claire looked up at Megan with tears in her eyes. "Just like us."

"Here's hoping not exactly like you two," their brother said drolly.

Claire sniffed and smiled up at Grunt. "Next time, we have to have girls."

"Sons *and* daughters. I like that." Grunt's face softened as he leaned forward to kiss his wife.

"Next time?" Megan looked around the room, and everyone seemed just as shocked as she felt.

"We're going to need a better plan," Lake said.

"And perhaps a different hospital," the doctor muttered.

Grunt lifted his head from his wife and beamed at everyone. "I'm a father," he announced again, then frowned. "When did you all get here?"

As everyone groaned, Megan hooked her arm through Dimitri's. "Okay," she whispered, her eyes on the babies. "I'll think about it."

The smile he gave her made her concession worthwhile. It also made her want to get out of there and practice for their future. Their *distant* future. While everyone explained to Grunt why they were so beaten up, Megan and Dimitri slipped out of the room. But not before she grabbed her go-bag.

Who knew when she'd need it again.

The Day Donna Became Housekeeper at Kintyre Mansion

It was common knowledge around Campbeltown that the owner of Kintyre Mansion was getting rid of staff left, right and center. Which meant he had vacancies, and Donna Sinclair was just desperate enough to apply for one of them.

"Are you sure about this?" her older sister Agnes asked as they drove up the sweeping drive to the imposing Georgian mansion. "This guy is notoriously hard to work for. He's fired six people in the past month alone."

"He's only lashing out because he's in pain." Duncan Stewart had lost his young wife a few months earlier, after a lengthy battle with cancer, and by all accounts, he wasn't coping well. "People need to have a little patience with him."

"No, they don't," her youngest sister, Mairi, said from the backseat. "What people need to do is keep far, far away until he's done grieving and stops lashing out. Seriously. Would you go near a lion with a thorn in its paw? No. Because you'd get your head bitten off. Self-preservation is how the species survives."

"You forget who you're talking to," Agnes said. "If there

were an injured lion within a two-hundred-mile radius, Donna would want to cuddle it until its boo-boo was healed."

"I would not. You guys always paint me as some sort of bleeding heart. I'm not, you know. I can be just as hard as the next person."

Agnes and Mairi burst out laughing.

"Say that again," Mairi said as she held up her phone. "I need to film it for Isobel. She'll be gutted she's stuck at home with the kids and missed it."

"Funny, very funny." Donna frowned at them, but her attention was stolen by the sight of the Georgian mansion house as it came into view. It looked like a massive stone cube with windows. There were three stories, with the windows on the top floor being smaller than those on the other two. There was an equal number of windows on either side of the vast front door and a sweeping stone staircase leading up to it —complete with wrought iron handrail.

"It looks very. . ." *Intimidating? Scary? Haunted?* "Grand," she said at last.

"Are you sure you want to do this?" Agnes said.

"We need the money, Aggie." That was the understatement of the year.

The four sisters pooled every penny they made to cover Agnes' university tuition and to pay off the loan Isobel's ex-husband had taken out—with a guy who broke legs if he didn't get his money.

"I'm earning now." As usual, Mairi was texting as she talked. "I can take on another couple of online boyfriends and up my hourly rate. You don't need to work for the Devil of Kintyre. You can wait and find a decent job in town."

Donna let out a sigh. Her eyes still fixed on the imposing building. Georgian architects sure liked symmetry. "I appreciate that. I do. But jobs are hard to come by right now. I haven't seen another vacancy in a bank since my branch closed down."

"Recession." Mairi gave a knowing nod.

"It isn't *recession*, dimwit," Agnes said. "It's the fact we live in the middle of nowhere. The only way off the peninsular is by boat or a five-hour drive to Glasgow. It isn't exactly a commutable location."

"Remind me," Mairi said sarcastically. "Why do we live here again?"

"Because our parents thought the world ended at the borders of Kintyre and we can't afford to move anywhere else," Agnes told her for the millionth time.

"And Isobel needs help with the kids," Donna added.

"It sucks being us." Mairi took a photo of the mansion to send to her fake boyfriends.

As Agnes parked the car in front of the stairs leading up to the main entrance, Donna took a deep breath. "Here we go. How do I look?"

"Like you could clean a house," Mairi said, "which is good, since that's the job you're applying for."

"Thanks." Donna climbed out of the car. "Helpful as usual."

Mairi beamed at her. "Knock 'em dead."

"And we'll help bury the body." Agnes gave her a thumbs up.

With a shake of her head and a smile, Donna climbed the curved steps to the main door. The gray cube of a building was severe, and she couldn't help but feel intimidated. But they did need the money, and beggars couldn't be choosers. Plus, the owner of the mansion was fast running out of staff who would put up with his mood swings. Donna figured if she could live with her three sisters, she could cope with one grieving man. All he needed was a little understanding and compassion. She could do that. Heck, she'd been born to do it.

She knocked on the door, stamping her feet against the cold as she waited for the housekeeper to answer. Living on the flattest part of the peninsular meant there was nothing to stop the winter winds as they came off the Atlantic and rushed straight through Campbeltown—as well as everyone who lived there. It was only the beginning of winter, and already Donna felt like she'd never get warm again.

As she waited for the housekeeper, she looked out over the mansion estate. At over fifty acres, the Kintyre holding was one of the largest in the area. And it looked a bit unkempt. The grass was barren in patches, bushes needed trimming, and the roses that lined the driveway were growing wild. If she didn't know better, she would have thought the place had been recently abandoned. There was a definite air of neglect hanging over the mansion—probably due to the owner losing the staff needed to care for it.

A noise drew her attention back to the vast oak door. Bolts turned with an ominous clang, making her think of every old *Hammer Horror* movie she'd watched as a child. Slowly, the door swung open, and Donna's jaw dropped. Because it wasn't the long-time housekeeper who appeared before her; it was the famed artist who owned the mansion.

"What do you want?" He glared at her as he folded his arms over his crinkled blue tartan shirt.

It was impossible to reply, because she was looking at the sexiest man she'd ever set eyes on. Even with a scowl on his face, Duncan Stewart was everything a man should be— rugged, masculine, strong. He wasn't a scrawny man, there were muscles under his clothes, and even barefoot he towered over her. Although, to be fair, most people towered over her. His hair was unkempt, his beard ragged, and deep lines were etched into his face. The kind of lines that came with agony rather than time. He oozed power, arrogance, and pain. And it was the pain that jerked Donna out of her daze. It was a stark reminder that he'd buried his young wife just a few months earlier.

"If you don't have anything to say, you can clear off. I don't have time for this." He made a move to swing the door shut in her face.

"Wait! I've come to see the housekeeper about the cleaning job."

He paused, staring at her with eyes so dark they seemed almost black. "I fired the housekeeper."

"Oh." She hadn't expected that. Although, given the rate he was going through staff, she probably should have. "Okay, well, who do I talk to about the job?"

His gaze seemed to bore right through her, and she found herself fighting the urge to squirm. She knew she wasn't much to look at. At just over five feet tall, with curves that betrayed a fondness for cake and a distinct disinterest in sport, she was the kind of woman who blended into the scenery. She had no standout features to redeem her. Her eyes were a watery green, her hair a mousy brown—with a kink in it that couldn't be bothered turning into a wave, and her nose a round dot in the middle of her face. A clown's nose. She'd often thought that if she'd painted the end red, people would think it was fake.

"You're hired," Duncan snapped once he'd finished his mysterious assessment.

"Thanks?" She couldn't hide her hesitance. "When do I start?"

"Now." He swung the door wide. "You're the new housekeeper." He grabbed a set of keys from the table beside the door. "Your apartment's on the third floor. It's included in the job. And there's a car somewhere." He scratched a beard that sorely needed trimming. "Ask the cook, she'll know." He turned back to the dark interior, clearly done with their conversation.

"Wait," Donna called. "I don't know anything about being a housekeeper, and you don't know anything about me. You didn't even ask my name. I came here for the cleaning job."

"There's more money in the housekeeping position, and I don't need a cleaner. Housekeeper's the only job I'm offering. Take it or leave it." His tone was flat, and his eyes were dead. It was clear he didn't care either way whether she took the job or walked away.

Donna knew her sisters would have taken one look at Duncan and run for the hills. The man was clearly on a course set for destruction, and there was a good chance he'd take down anyone near him when he went. But she couldn't get past the agony in his eyes. Inside, he was screaming and wailing, raging against his grief and loss. He was lost, and there was no one around to help him find his way back. He'd fired most of the mansion staff, and it was well known around town that he refused to see his friends and family. He'd isolated himself while letting his grief slowly kill him. He needed someone, anyone, to look out for him. How could she walk away from a need like that?

She took a deep breath. "My name is Donna Sinclair. My record is clean. I don't drink, smoke, or do drugs."

"Like I said, you're hired." He pointed to the stairs. "Find your own way."

"That's it? No job description? No contract?"

"I'll email my lawyer. She'll sort out a contract and your wages. The job description's easy—keep everybody out of my way and finish my wife's renovations." He stalked away but turned before the gloom of the building swallowed him. "And no damn parties." With that, he was gone.

Donna stood there for a moment, wondering what had just happened. She'd come for a part-time position and nabbed a full-time live-in job—with a man who was broken and hitting out at everyone around him. On reflection, it might have been a good idea to turn down the job and call in the professionals to deal with Duncan.

"Is he gone?" Mairi came up behind her and peered into the foyer.

"Yeah." Donna looked in the direction Duncan had disappeared.

"Did you get the job?" Agnes said over Mairi's shoulder.

She forced a smile. "You're looking at Kintyre Mansion's new housekeeper."

"*Housekeeper?*"

Donna tried hard to look like she was happy about her new job, when mainly what she felt was terror at biting off more than she could chew. But still...Duncan Stewart needed *somebody*. She took a deep breath and forced a smile. "Apparently it's a live-in position. There's a flat on the third floor."

"Cool," Mairi said. "A live-in housekeeper makes more money, right?"

"Dingbat." Agnes smacked her youngest sister on the back of her head. "You only ever think about the money."

"We're poor, Aggie. What else are we supposed to think about?"

"Well, you could try thinking about the fact Donna will be living here all alone with a strange man. One who has a reputation for being bad-tempered."

"Oh, that." Mairi's eyes widened, and she brushed her mane of wild, red curls from her face. "Maybe we should stay here with you for a few days, just to make sure he isn't an axe murderer or something."

"Good idea." Donna didn't like the look of the huge, empty house, and the thought of staying there alone with the grieving widower didn't appeal to her at all.

"Did you even want this job?" Agnes said.

"I'm sure it's a great job." Donna sidestepped the question but fooled nobody.

"Oh, Donna," Agnes sighed. "You did it again, didn't you? You saw a lost cause and you couldn't say no."

"He needs someone to look out for him," Donna protested. "How was I supposed to say no to that? He's just lost his wife."

"And gained a housekeeper who doesn't know anything about the job," Agnes added. "One who's too soft-hearted and easy to walk over."

"I resent that." Donna glared at her.

Agnes lifted her hand and ticked off on her fingers. "You're a member of the Bacon of the Month Club, even though you're vegetarian, because the guy was worried that he'd lose his job if he didn't sign people up. You once spent a weekend at a Jehovah's Witness retreat because you felt sorry for them not being able to talk people into going along. You—"

"Enough." Donna held up her hand to stop the long, embarrassing list. "I need a job. Duncan needs a housekeeper."

"Or a keeper generally," Mairi said helpfully.

Donna frowned at her. "This is decent money. And a good job in an economy where there aren't many. It also means I can move out of Isobel's house, so she'll have more space for her and the kids. He even said there was a car I could use. I don't see a downside." What she really meant was that she didn't *want* to see the downside.

"The big, angry, grief-stricken guy who keeps firing people might be the downside," Agnes said. "He's hell to work for. He's got a temper, and he isn't afraid to use it."

"I can cope with shouting." Donna didn't need to remind them that their dad had been an expert in that area. "He just looked so sad, what was I supposed to do? Say no? He really needs a housekeeper."

"Because he fired the last one," Agnes guessed, making Donna wince.

"I don't know why you're giving her a hard time about this," Mairi said. "If she can't say no to bacon, she didn't have a hope in hell of turning down a sad sack like Duncan Stewart. On the plus side, if the job's horrible, she probably won't be in it long. He'll most likely fire her before the week's out. Now, can we go see the housekeeper's accommodation? And a wee tour of the rest of the house would be nice too. I've always wanted to check this place out. Although, it's creepier than it looks from the outside." She turned to her sisters. "Are we sure his wife died? I mean, she isn't locked in the attic, right?"

"Mairi!" Donna poked her sister in the ribs.

Mairi held up her hands. "Just asking."

And together the three sisters headed up the wide, curved stairway to Donna's new accommodation.

Megan and Dimitri on the Job

"I swear, if she puts her hands on you one more time," Megan said through gritted teeth, "I'm cutting them off."

Dimitri smiled indulgently at his fiancée. "She doesn't mean anything by it, Buffy. It's just her way."

Megan's head turned slowly as she pinned him with a fiery stare. "*It's just her way?*"

"Yeah." He shrugged, feeling the weight of his sidearm in its shoulder holster. "She's one of those touchy-feely types. Most actresses are."

Oh yeah, her eyes were definitely flashing fire now. "She doesn't touch me."

"That's because of those scary vibes you give off. I'm more of a laid-back kind of guy, more approachable." He fought to keep his face blank. "More touchable. I don't mind. I get it a lot."

For a second, he could have sworn there was steam coming out of her ears. "*You don't mind?*"

Man, she was stunning when she was jealous. She was also dangerous. You never quite knew what Megan Donaldson was going to do next, and now she had a permit to carry a firearm, that made teasing her a risky business. Which meant, he probably shouldn't do it, no matter how much fun it was.

"Buffy," he said softly, "I don't want anyone but you to touch me."

Her mood shifted from jealous outrage to sexual possession at the flip of a switch. Her blue eyes pinned him in place as she closed the distance between them to stand in front of him. A short, unvarnished fingernail trailed down the front of his black dress shirt.

"That's good," she said as she leaned into him, making every inch of his body scream to be touched. "Because only I get to touch you." She stepped back, resuming her position on the other side of the hotel suite's doorway. "Which is what I'm going to tell Princess Pain-in-the-arse as soon as her meeting's finished."

It was clear the only way to stop her would be to tie her to their bed. Unfortunately, that wasn't an option, so he went for reason. "Remember, she's a *paying* client. This new service of Rachel's offers women a safe and secure experience with Benson Security. We're supposed to make women feel comfortable while we protect them."

Her chin went up, making her blonde ponytail bob. "That doesn't mean we pander to the clients. I can guard her body a whole lot better when she isn't touching yours."

There was no talking sense to her. She was determined to have it out with the Hollywood actress who'd hired them to protect her. All he could do now was damage control. Which made him grin—life with Megan would never be boring, and he couldn't wait to marry her. Only seventeen more days and then he could relax, knowing he'd tied her to him forever. Until then, he had to live with the worry of her being free to walk away.

Over his dead body!

Megan caught his frown and rolled her eyes. "You're thinking about our wedding again, aren't you? Or more precisely, how you can get me down the aisle faster."

There was no denying it. "I have a license. We could go to the courthouse after our shift ends."

"This is London. There's no going to the courthouse. We have our weddings in churches or at the registrar's office, which is generally located in some concrete monstrosity built in the seventies that looks like it should house serial offenders." She cocked an eyebrow at him. "Not exactly my idea of romance."

"I don't care about romance. I care about getting a ring on your finger and a signature on a document that makes it harder for you to leave me."

"You are so insecure." She shook her head in disgust. "If you didn't have a fantastic six-pack and thighs like tree trunks, I would totally leave you."

It was comments like that made him want to drag her ass in front of the nearest judge—damn it, *registrar*. If they were in the US, this wouldn't be an issue; he'd have her in Vegas so fast that her head would spin. He wondered if that was an option. No, unfortunately, they were on the job, and they couldn't walk off without leaving their client wide open to an attack by her secret admirer slash stalker. Which reminded him. "Did you get a look at the latest threatening letter? It looked kinda hinky to me."

"No. Rachel whisked it away for analysis before I had a chance." She glanced around the corridor. "Would it kill them to provide us with a couple of stools? My feet are aching. How long does one meeting with your agent take? What is there to talk about? *You're a crap actress. No one wants you. I'll call if they do.* That takes, what? Ten seconds to say."

"She isn't a crap actress. She's just has a limited *breadth* of performance." He'd heard that from Belinda, who was an amazing actress, and thought it made him sound knowl-edgeable.

Megan wasn't fooled. "Stop reading *Variety*. It's messing with your head."

"I didn't get that from *Variety*."

"Well, stop listening to Belinda. Our charge can't act." She paused. "And ninety percent of her body's been put together by Silicon Inc. Lips, tits, arse. There's so much plastic in her, she won't biodegrade for centuries after she's buried."

Glenn Close's voice suddenly blared out, saying her famous line from *Fatal Attraction*, 'I'm not going to be *ignored*, Dan.' Megan pulled her phone out of her blazer pocket.

"Rachel." She groaned.

"You'd better hope she never hears her ringtone," Dimitri said.

"Like Rachel scares me," she scoffed as she swiped the screen. "Wassup?" she said to their boss. There was a pause while she listened, and then, "No, I can't put you on speaker, we're in the corridor, guarding the freaking door. I can fill Dim Boy in after we're done."

His eyes ate her up as she listened to Rachel. Even in a plain black pant suit and white dress shirt, she was still the sexiest woman he'd ever set eyes on. And he wasn't the only one who noticed. Everywhere they went, men craned their necks to get a better look at her. Hell, she got more attention than the actress they were protecting. It was probably the reason Samantha kept touching him—she was jealous of Megan. He needed to talk to Rachel about the situation. Megan guarding the actress wasn't working. She needed to assign a different team.

"Sure we'll wait for you before we talk to her," Megan said, her tone unnaturally casual, which set off all sorts of alarm bells. "How far away are you? Ten minutes? Fantastic. See you then." She shut the phone off, slid it into her pocket, and turned toward the door.

Dimitri's hand shot out, grabbing her arm to stop her. "What was that about? Aren't you meant to wait for Rachel to get here before you talk to Samantha?"

"Oh, I think I need to have a word with our charge right now." She shook off his hold, threw open the door, and stormed into the suite.

Although he knew better than to get between a Scottish woman and the object of her fury, duty demanded he at least follow and try to contain her. It was like trying to contain a tornado. She strode along the short hallway and turned left into the living-room area. As soon as they entered the room, Samantha shot to her feet while her agent—spray tan in a suit—shoved a set of papers into his briefcase, in a move so fast and practiced, Dimitri wasn't even sure he'd seen it.

"What are you doing in here?" Samantha snapped. "This is a private meeting. Surely you didn't think my own agent was a threat? And who's guarding the door? What if someone sneaks in while you aren't watching? This is my life on the line."

"No. It's not." Megan strode toward the actress, forcing her back into her seat just by her presence.

"Maybe I should go." The agent stood.

"Sit!" Megan snapped.

The man froze, unsure of what to do. Dimitri might be in the dark about the situation, but he sure as hell was going to back Megan up.

"You heard her," he ordered. "Sit."

The man sat.

"I'll have you fired for this," Samantha said. "Rachel will be furious with the way you treat her clients."

"Funny you should mention Rachel." Megan folded her arms and spread her feet wide as she stood in front of the actress. "I just got off the phone with her, and she has some concerns about this supposed stalker of yours."

The woman paled, her hands shaking as her shoulders went back. She lifted her chin and stared down her nose at Megan. "Well, I'm sure Rachel will discuss them with me later. Now, please leave and let us finish our meeting."

Dimitri sighed. Megan was right; the woman couldn't act worth a damn. It was clear she was nervous and did very much care about whatever Rachel had told Megan.

"I'm calling your boss." The agent dug his phone out of his pocket. "This is unacceptable."

Megan reached over, snatched the phone from his hands and tossed it over her shoulder.

"That's it!" The agent shot to his feet. "I won't stand for this."

"You're right. You won't." Megan reached for her hip, unsnapped her holster, pulled out her gun and aimed it straight at the man's forehead. "Sit," she ordered the man. He sat. "Stay," she added. And there was no doubt in anyone's mind that he would stay.

And just like that, the situation had spiraled down the toilet.

"Eh, Buffy?" Dimitri kept his eyes on the two people they were supposed to be protecting but were now threatening. "Want to get me up to speed here?"

"Don't worry, babe" she said, her gun still trained on the agent. "It will soon become clear." Her arm swung the weapon to point it at Samantha's head. "Keep an eye on the overgrown Oompa Loompa for me while I have a talk with Princess Pain-in-the-arse."

"Well, I never..." Samantha started to complain, but was silenced by the sight of a gun aimed at the spot between her eyes.

"As I was saying," Megan said. "I just got off the phone

with Rachel, and she told me something really interesting. It seems there was a fingerprint match on the last threatening letter you received. Want to guess whose it was?"

There was silence as Samantha and her agent shared a glance. And it was enough to tell Dimitri the whole story—they'd been had.

"No?" Megan said, her hand steady as she kept the gun pointed at Samantha's head. "It was yours. We found your print on the letter."

"Well, of course you did." Samantha shifted in her seat, smiling benignly. "I opened it."

"Did you also put the stamp on it? Because the print was halfway under the stamp."

The agent jerked to his feet and ran for the door, holding his briefcase in front of him like a battering ram. Dimitri shot out his arm and clotheslined the guy. A second later, the man lay on the floor, holding his throat and gasping for air.

"My fiancée told you to stay," Dimitri said as he flipped the man onto his front. "She gets upset when people don't do as she says. And when she gets upset, it upsets me." He secured the man's hands behind his back with zip ties.

"Thanks, Dim Boy." Megan blew him a kiss.

"You're both insane." Samantha's eyes were wide with shock.

"And you can't act worth a damn." Dimitri picked up the briefcase and opened it. It was filled with threatening letters, ones they'd obviously been working on during their meeting. "Yet, it's still better than your criminal efforts." He held up the letters. "How could you think you'd get away with this?" He looked at Megan. "I feel like I'm in an episode of *Scooby-Doo*."

"I'll give you a Scooby snack later. Once I've finished talking to this idiot." She looked back at the actress. "Lesson one—all the publicity in the world won't improve your acting.

Lesson two—if you ever put your hands on Dimitri again, I will remove them."

"So much for waiting," Rachel said from the doorway, her upper-class English accent sounding cold as ice. "Megan, please don't shoot Samantha. The bill from the hotel to remove the blood stains from the carpet would cripple Benson Security."

Rachel glided into the room on black designer pumps with bright red soles. She wore a black bespoke skirt suit and held her ever-present iPhone in her manicured hand. Red fingernails tapped at the phone as she gave the actress an icy stare.

"This isn't how I do business, Samantha," she said coldly.

As interrogation techniques went, Rachel's was more about inflicting mental distress than physical pain, but it usually worked. As Samantha proved when she crumpled. "I needed the publicity, my career—"

"You don't have a career," Rachel said. "Not anymore." Her thumb flicked over the screen of her phone. "The police are on their way." With a dismissive toss of her long dark hair, she turned to Megan, who still had her gun aimed at Samantha's head. "What did I say about guns?"

With a sigh, Megan put the gun away. "Rach, you say a lot of stuff. How am I supposed to remember it all? Plus, I didn't shoot her. Although, I really, really wanted to." She looked back at Samantha as though she were still considering it. "There aren't many places I could aim for on her body where the bullet wouldn't hit rubber and just bounce off."

She was magnificent, in a slightly deranged, blood-thirsty kind of way.

"Man, I love you," Dimitri said.

"For the love of all things Prada," Rachel said. "We're at work. Keep your relationship for your own time."

She had a point.

As the police came through the door, Dimitri put an arm around Megan's shoulders and guided her away from Samantha, just in case she snapped and did something they'd both regret.

"I really didn't like her touching you," she said as she tried to stare holes through the actress.

"I know, Buffy, I know." He lifted her chin and kissed her hard.

"For the love of Gucci," Rachel shouted. "Not on the job!"

Reluctantly, Dimitri broke the kiss. "Only seventeen more days until you become Megan Raast."

"If you're lucky," the evil woman said.

The Wookiee Wants a Wife (or at the very least, a date!)

Jonas Tremblay paced the vast interior of his penthouse apartment. This was a mistake. A humungous mistake. He couldn't go on a blind date. He could barely leave his apartment. And if he did, he broke out in a cold sweat if he wasn't wearing his Wookiee costume. And he couldn't wear his Wookiee suit on a date.

Could he?

No. No, he couldn't.

Which meant he couldn't go. He'd just have to call Mairi, thank her for setting this up for him, and hang up on her before she could talk him into anything else. Or send her a text. Or an email. Or a coded message that would take her a couple of weeks to decode, and by then, he'd be living in a hut in the Yukon, keeping the moose company and wearing his Wookiee costume to blend with the grizzly bears. No, even that wouldn't work. The wilderness didn't have any internet. Which meant he was going to die alone in his big, empty, expensive apartment, looking out over Montreal and all the people living their normal lives in a normal way, without him.

He bent over, put his hands on his knees, and took several

slow breaths. His hands shook as dizziness and nausea rose in a wave, and the walls closed in on him. Two thousand square feet of living space and it was suffocating.

Good job there wasn't much furniture to trip over while he paced. Even though he'd been out of college for almost a decade, he'd furnished the place in student chic—TV, sofa, bed, stocked fridge and a shit-ton of computer equipment. There was nothing else except a vast expanse of marble tiling and white walls. And a view over Montreal's Mount Royal. Yeah, he'd bought a condo in the middle of the Golden Square Mile. Because he didn't know what else to do with his money, and a multi-million-dollar pad had seemed like a good idea at the time. He was pathetic. And he hated his condo.

He hated his life.

He hated himself.

Why couldn't he just be normal? But no, he had to have a giant brain and a deep fear of other human beings. Unless he was online. Which was how he'd gotten into this mess in the first place—he'd hired a virtual girlfriend to keep him company and make him feel normal. But then he'd thought himself in love and had flown to Scotland, dressed as a Wookiee—not his finest moment—to meet his virtual girlfriend, Mairi, in real life and win her hand in marriage. Of course, she hadn't wanted him or any of the other sad geeks who'd turned up. But pity had made her offer to find him the perfect match. And his love for Mairi had meant he let her.

Which had led to this moment. Forty-five minutes until he was due downstairs to meet his blind date in the hotel bar. Now, he was just going to text Mairi.

And hide.

For the rest of his life.

His doorbell rang, ruining that plan. There were only three people his doorman let up to his apartment: his parents and his best friend, Sebastian. He knew which one was at his door. And he wouldn't go away until Jonas let him in.

With a sigh, he threw the door open for his friend. Sebastian stood there, on the phone, glaring up at Jonas while he talked.

"You were right," he said. "He's freaking out. Here." He thrust the phone into Jonas' hand.

With a sinking heart, he took it, knowing full well who was on the other end. "I can't do it," he said as soon as it reached his ear.

"Yes. You can." Mairi's Scottish accent filled his head. "And you will. Or I will get on a plane, come over there to Canada, and beat you to within an inch of your life."

"Rusty," Mairi's fiancé, Keir, called in the background. "We talked about how you treat your clients. That isn't the way."

"Jonas isn't a client," Mairi snapped. "He's Jonas. Now butt out. Do I tell you how to fix cars? No, I don't. So don't tell me how to fix my geeks."

It was probably all kinds of weird that Jonas felt warm inside being called one of Mairi's geeks, but he did.

"Right," she said, all business now she'd dealt with Keir. "You've talked to Sadie online. You've exchanged photos—without the Wookiee head, thank goodness. You know this woman. It's not like you're meeting a stranger. It will be fine."

"Yeah." He shook his head. "No, it won't. I can't do it."

"Dude," Sebastian shouted. "Man up."

Jonas flipped him the bird. Sebastian just grinned then turned to raid his fridge.

"Jonas William Tremblay, you will get yourself downstairs and spend at least half an hour face to face with Sadie Carlyle. Do you hear me?"

"Yeah, I hear you. How can I not when you're shouting in

my ear? You're also in Scotland, so your threat doesn't hold water."

"Really? You think I can't carry out a threat from a few million—"

"Thousand," Jonas said.

"Thousand," Mairi corrected without missing a beat, "miles away?"

"Don't risk it," Keir called in the background. "She'll totally keep her word and screw with your life."

"Tell Keir I have no life for you to screw with," Jonas said.

"You would do if you'd just get your backside down to the hotel restaurant. We picked this location to help make you feel comfortable. You live in the damn hotel. You know the restaurant. If the date goes sideways, you can get in the lift and go back upstairs."

"I don't live in the hotel. I bought one of the hotel's residencies added on to the original building. Technically, I live *hotel adjacent*."

There was a pause, and he knew if Mairi had been in front of him, her face would have been as red as her hair, which would have been his signal to run. "Do you get room service?" she demanded. "Can you use the hotel housekeeping?"

"Uh, yeah." It was his turn to turn red, but it wasn't from anger.

"Then you're living in the freaking hotel!" she shouted, before muttering, "Deep breath, take a deep breath."

Jonas hit the mute button and glared at his friend, who was now eating leftover pizza while lounging on the black leather couch. Yeah, he was that much of a cliché. He'd bought black leather because he was a guy who didn't know what else to buy. And because you could wipe beer off it.

"You set Mairi on me?" he demanded.

Sebastian shrugged. "She phoned me. She was shouting before I even said hello, convinced that you were holed up in here, hiding from your date. She wasn't wrong." He shook his head in disgust.

"Jonas! Are you there?" the phone screeched.

He unmuted it and put it to his ear. "Yeah, I'm still here. And I'm really sorry, Mairi, but I can't go on this date. I can't go on any dates. Your services are no longer needed because I've resolved to die a lonely old man."

"Of for goodness' sake. That's it. You have only yourself to blame for what happens next." With that, the phone went dead.

He stared at it for a minute before tossing it onto the sofa beside Sebastian. "She hung up on me," he said.

Sebastian's eyes went wide. "Oh, you're in trouble now."

"Probably. But let's face it, there isn't a whole lot she can do from Scotland." He headed for his laptop, which was sitting on the breakfast counter that divided the kitchen from the rest of his open-plan living space. "I need to tell Sadie and tell her the date's off."

"You're an idiot. That girl is cute."

Sebastian wasn't wrong. Jonas brought up the photo Sadie had sent him. She'd taken it at work, surrounded by the smiling old folk she helped. She was an art therapist, working for several nursing homes throughout the city, and she loved her job. And, if the smiles of the people she was with were anything to go by, the job loved her too.

He trailed a fingertip over the outline of her face. She had a perfectly oval face, with exactly the same number of freckles each side of her nose. He'd counted. And if that made him even weirder, he could live with it. Her golden hair sat in a messy bun on top of her head, her eyes were a pale green, and her top lip looked significantly thinner than the bottom one. He hadn't measured to be sure. Although, he'd wanted to.

Sebastian was right; she was cute. She was also outgoing,

funny, and full of life—the exact opposite of Jonas. What did he have to offer her? How could they date when he even struggled to talk to his doorman? And he'd known him for years. Crippling shyness and social anxiety. That was the definition of his particular brand of weird. And the older he got, the worse it became. He'd been joking about spending the rest of his life locked in his apartment alone. But he feared it was closer to the truth than he liked to admit.

He opened his email and typed his apologies. There was no point in making excuses. How did you explain you were terrified of meeting someone face to face? When he was done, he shut the laptop and headed for the fridge.

"Want a beer?" he asked Sebastian.

His friend frowned at him. "What I want is for you to put on your shoes and go downstairs to meet the pretty girl."

"I've called it off. She won't be there even if a miracle happens and I make it out of the apartment." He grabbed two bottle of beer and headed over to the armchair beside his friend.

Night had fallen over Montreal, and the lights of the city blinked through the floor-to-ceiling windows that made up a wall of his apartment.

"I don't get it." Sebastian took the offered beer. "What's keeping you in here? I mean, look at you. You're classically handsome, and I say that as an enlightened metro-male and not because I'm into you. You're rich, you're smart, you know a ton of useful trivia, and you're a huge *Star Wars* fan. You've got it going on, man. You could have any woman you wanted. But instead, you're stuck in here, drinking beer with me, while your date finds a backup. What are you so scared of? What's keeping you from living it up?"

"If I knew the answer to that, you'd be sitting here alone."

He'd had therapy. *All* the therapies—cognitive, group, and exposure. He'd taken medication to relieve anxiety, but all it'd done was make him fall asleep or puke. He'd tried meditation, flotation tanks, acupuncture and about a million other things that he thought might cure him. The truth of the matter was, he was naturally shy to begin with, and having social anxiety on top of that made it even more difficult to face the world. Unless he was hiding—online, or in costume—social situations made him panic or pass out. Although, dressing as a Wookiee helped a bit. At least in his costume, he didn't have to talk. He just opened his mouth and a warble came out.

His doorbell rang as he took as sip of his beer, making him swallow the wrong way and almost choke to death. Of the three people allowed to come straight up to his door, one of them was already inside his apartment.

"Dude," Sebastian said with sympathy, "she called your mom."

The doorbell rang again, reminding Jonas of one of the downsides of living in a hotel. If he'd been in a regular apartment block, and hadn't given his mother a key, she wouldn't be able to get in. But in his block, all she had to do was call down to housekeeping and someone would open the door for her. She'd done it before when he'd been working on a game design for days straight and she was worried he'd died.

She'd walked in to find him sitting in his underpants, and nothing else, eating Cheerios from the box on his breakfast bar while tapping at the keyboard on his laptop. He hadn't showered or combed his hair in days.

"Oh good," his mother had said. "You're alive. Although, you smell like a dead body."

It had gone downhill from there.

"I'd better get it," he said with a sigh.

"Mairi's evil." Sebastian shook his head. "You should have just done as you were told. Now, you're going to suffer."

Shooting a glare at his friend, Jonas headed for the door and threw it open.

It wasn't his mother.

It was an Ewok.

The Ewok looked up at him with human eyes. "Aren't we doing costumes? I thought you'd be dressed as a Wookiee. Now I feel overdressed." The Ewok held up a phone. "Mairi said to come on up, that you were too nervous to meet in public. I totally get it. I was a bit nervous about meeting face to face for the first time too. Although, the costume helps. You were right about that."

"Sadie?" Jonas said.

"Sorry." The Ewok giggled and stuck out a paw. "Nice to meet you in person."

Stunned, and more than slightly bewildered, Jonas shook the offered paw.

"Ewoks don't carry lightsabers," he said inanely.

"Oh, right." She held it out to him. "I was hoping you'd take a look at it. The noises are all wrong, and you said you were technical. Is it the wrong type of technical? Did I make a mistake? I should have left it at home."

"No!" He took the lightsaber. "I can look at it."

"Great." She shuffled her furry feet. "I have cupcakes too. It's kind of dumb, I know, bringing cupcakes to a fancy hotel. But I make great cupcakes. These are caramel. You like caramel, right? I mean, everybody likes caramel. Don't they?"

A voice shouted from behind him, "Invite her in, dumbass." Reminding Jonas that Sebastian was still there.

Sadie giggled again, those pale eyes of hers sparkling from behind her fuzzy mask. Jonas couldn't say another word; he'd been struck dumb by her appearance. He just swung the door wide and motioned her inside. Then watched in bewilderment as she waddled into his home. A cute little fuzzy teddy bear with a massive round belly and a pink shopping bag full of cupcakes.

"I'm Sebastian; I was just leaving," his friend said as he

stood. "And you're an Ewok. Cool costume. Did I hear you say cupcakes?"

"Would you like one?" the Ewok, no, Sadie, said.

"If there's enough," replied the greedy pig, practically drooling.

As Sebastian reached for the bag, his phone rang. He glanced at the display. "It's for you," he told Jonas as he tossed the phone at him.

Jonas had followed Sadie into his living room, feeling somewhat dazed as he did so. He snatched the phone out of the air and looked at the screen. Surprise, surprise, it was Mairi.

"Please tell me you've let her into the apartment?" she said when he answered the call.

Jonas turned his back on the people in his home. "How did you get her past the front desk?"

"I'm not telling you. Now be nice to that woman." There was a pause. "You still like her, right?"

The note of uncertainty in Mairi's voice unnerved him. "She dressed as an Ewok for our date," he whispered.

"You *more* than like her," Mairi said with a smile in her voice. "I'll call later for a debrief. Just be yourself, Jonas. You're perfect just the way you are." And with that, she hung up.

"I'm out of here," Sebastian said as he passed him, a cupcake in his hand. He took his phone from Jonas. "I like her. And she makes great cupcakes." With a waggle of his eyebrows and a knowing smile, Sebastian disappeared into the foyer. The sound of the door closing behind him reverberated through the almost empty apartment. Jonas was alone with his blind date.

And, strangely enough, he didn't feel anxious about it. He was on his home turf, and she'd dressed up, just for him.

Slowly, he made his way into the kitchen area and found her trying to unload cupcakes with two furry paws for hands.

"Let me." He took the bag from her and placed the cakes on a plate.

"Shouldn't I have come up here?" Sadie said through her mask. "Mairi said it was okay."

"Mairi was meddling, which is kind of what she's supposed to do."

They lapsed into silence, but it wasn't as uncomfortable as it probably should have been.

"I sent you an email." Jonas felt he had to confess before she read it. "I called off our date."

"Oh." The Ewok looked at the floor. "I guess I'd better leave then."

"No." He reached out and took her paw in his hand, feeling strangely confident as he did so. "I'm glad you're here. It's like I explained online. I get...anxious."

His face burned at the confession. Aware that, at six-foot tall and with more muscles than your average geek (which, he really should have printed on a T-shirt), he wasn't exactly the poster child for anxiety disorders. It was embarrassing.

"I understand," Sadie said. "Really, I do. I have to breathe into a paper bag at the dentist. And that's just for a checkup. If they have to do any treatments, I need to be knocked out."

"Yeah, but that's only at the dentist. I'm like this twenty-four seven."

"Don't underestimate how crippling dental fear can be," she said solemnly. "It got in the way of my career as a dental hygienist."

His lips quirked as laugher bubbled inside him. "I could see that being a problem."

She nodded. "All those years spent playing with dental Barbie, and it came to nothing."

"Dental Barbie?"

"Trust me, it's a thing."

Jonas took the first relaxed breath he'd taken in hours as he leaned against the counter. "Do you want to sit outside on the balcony and eat cupcakes?"

She cocked her fuzzy little head at him. "You sure you're ready for that? It would mean I'd have to take off my Ewok head and paws. I don't want to rush into the next step in our relationship too soon."

"And being decostumed is the next step?"

"It is if decostumed is a word."

He made a show of looking down at himself. "Looks like I'm already a step ahead of you then."

He was wearing his usual: faded jeans and a black printed T-shirt. This one had a floppy disk and a USB drive on it. The floppy's speech bubble said, "I am your father." And the USB's said, "Nooooo." He thought it was funny, but he'd have changed into a dress shirt for their date. It was too late now. Their date had already started.

"Since you're being forward," she said as she pulled off a paw, "I may as well catch up."

He watched with fascination as her slender hands appeared. And then, as those hands reached for her full-head mask. It was the geekiest striptease on the planet, and it made his heart race. Slowly, the smooth skin of her throat appeared, then the curve of her chin, followed by her tiny pointed nose, with all those freckles flanking it, and finally, her pale green eyes stared up into his. She placed the head on the counter in front of them. Her hair was in a messy bun, some strands standing on end from the static electricity of the costume. She was stunning.

As they stared at each other, her uneven lips broke into a beautiful wide smile, and she held out a human hand. "Hi, Jonas, I'm Sadie. It's lovely to meet you in person at last."

Jonas couldn't take his eyes from hers as he reached for

her hand. When they touched, a shock of pure electricity ran straight up his arm to his heart, and his mouth went dry. He swallowed hard as he smiled back at her.

"Hi, Sadie, I'm Jonas. It's lovely to meet you in person at last."

And then, they stood there, holding hands and staring at each other for what felt like an eternity. A perfect, wonderful, calm eternity.

Isobel And Callum Get Married

"I can't do it." Isobel doubled over and wedged her head between her knees in an attempt to ease the spinning in her head. It didn't work. Instead, all that happened was her dress tried to suffocate her.

"Why did I pick this dress?" She batted at the skirt, but it still remained voluminous. "What was I thinking? There's so much satin, it's eating me alive. And it's white. I can't wear white. I have two kids, an ex-husband and a teenage pregnancy in my past."

"I hate to break it to you, honey," her youngest sister, Mairi, said. "But the two kids aren't only in your past."

"Mum!" Her three-year-old shouted from where she was sitting in the corner of the room, drawing pictures. She held up her latest masterpiece and beamed.

"Very nice," Isobel said absently, and Sophie went back to her art.

The walls of the bedroom she shared with Callum were closing in on Isobel. The air growing thicker by the second. She had to get out. But her three sisters stood between her and the door. She jumped to her feet, gathered up her dress, and paced.

"This is a mistake. I shouldn't be getting married. I have a crap track record with relationships. What if Callum turns out to be just like Robert? What then? I've moved myself and my kids to London to live with him. What was I thinking? If this goes belly-up, we'll be homeless. I've risked the security of my children, just because I can't keep my pants on around the man. I'm a terrible mother!"

"Calm down," Agnes snapped. "Callum is nothing like Robert. He's honorable, and stable, and doesn't have a gambling habit."

"Hotter too," Mairi added.

"Scarier," Donna muttered from her perch on the arm of the sofa.

A sofa. *In her bedroom!* "Look at this place." Isobel waved her arm to indicate the room. "This one room is bigger than my last house."

"Is that really the most important thing to focus on right now?" Agnes tossed her blonde hair, folded her arms, and tapped her toe with growing frustration.

Isobel ignored her. Agnes had nothing to be irritated about. She wasn't the one getting married.

Married! What was she doing? He was so out of her league that it wasn't funny.

"He owns a successful business. He travels the world. He's got skills and an education." Isobel stomped across the polished wooden floor until she came to the wall, then she turned and stomped back again. "What do I have? Two kids. No money. No skills. Nothing. He's going to regret marrying me, and then he'll leave me." She pressed a hand to her suddenly roiling stomach. "I cannot have another failed relationship. I'm only thirty-three!"

"Maybe I should call Callum." Donna dug her phone out of her handbag.

"Don't you dare." Isobel glared at her, and Donna froze in place.

The last thing she needed was for Callum to see her in hysterics. He'd think he caused it. That she was having second thoughts because of his prosthetic legs. But Callum wasn't the problem. It was her. All her.

"I'm sure Callum would help." Donna's eyes grew wide as she held up a placating hand.

"I swear I will hurt you if you call him." Isobel wasn't sure how threatening she looked dressed as a meringue, but it didn't take much to intimidate her middle sister. As expected, Donna backed down.

"Oh for goodness' sake." Agnes strode over to Donna and snatched the phone from her hand. "Nobody's calling anyone. You"—she pointed at Donna—"are going to sit quietly while I deal with this. And you"—she pointed at Isobel—"are going to calm the hell down and remember you love the man you're marrying."

"Hell!" Sophie shouted from her corner.

"Great, now she's cursing." Isobel glared at Agnes who looked unrepentant.

Sophie, meanwhile, happily went back to coloring.

Isobel glared at her sisters. "This isn't about love. It's about marriage. I can't get married. I thought I could, but I can't." She tugged at the bodice of her dress. "I need to get out of this. I'm suffocating."

"No!" Agnes snapped. "We just got you into it."

Isobel was past listening. She clawed at the dress, popping the pearl buttons on the back that Donna had painstakingly fastened for her.

"Give me back my phone." Donna sounded hysterical. "I'm calling Callum."

"No. You're not," Agnes ordered. "She's just having a wobble."

Mairi burst out laughing. "Is that what we're calling it? If she's wobbling, then the two of you are wobbling right along with her."

Isobel tugged the dress over her hips, letting it fall to the floor, and stepped out of it. She bent, scooped it up, and threw it into the corner.

"Tent!" Sophie shouted and climbed into the dress.

"Not with your markers!" Agnes dove for her niece.

They all watched as Agnes fought to remove the giggling three-year-old from the dress.

"Anyone got stain remover?" Agnes said in disgust as she stood clutching Sophie. "The white dress now has pink graffiti."

Isobel stopped pacing long enough to look at her beaming daughter. At some point in the past five minutes, Sophie had decided she needed makeup and had added some to her face with her marker pens. A red scrawl covered her lips and cheeks, and there were two wonky blue circles around her eyes.

"See?" Isobel pointed at her. "Look at her face. Nothing's going right. It's a sign. The universe knows I shouldn't get married again!"

"Get a grip." Agnes removed the pens from the giggling three-year-old before she could draw on her face too. "This isn't a sign. It's hysterics." She handed Sophie to Mairi. "Can you clean her up?"

"Come here, gorgeous," Mairi said. "We'll take this off, and I'll let you play with some real makeup."

"No!" Agnes said.

Mairi rolled her eyes. "I was only going to give her the brushes. Seriously, give me some credit here. I'm not the one having a meltdown an hour before I'm due to get married."

Donna picked up the discarded wedding dress. "I could maybe clean this with some nail polish remover." She didn't sound hopeful.

Isobel didn't care. She needed to pace. And to rant. Nothing else mattered, and she seriously wished her sisters would bog off and let her get on with it.

The door crashed open, making three of the women squeal.

"Clam!" Sophie held out her arms to Callum.

"Later, my girl." He gave her a gentle smile. "I need to deal with your mum, and by the looks of things, you need to have your face washed."

Sophie giggled and ducked her head into Mairi's neck. It was then Isobel noticed Mairi wasn't surprised to see Callum standing in the doorway.

"Traitor!" Isobel pointed at her youngest sister. "You sent him a text."

Mairi shrugged. "Yep. I told him to get his arse up here and to bring some heavy sedation along with him." She looked up at Callum. "Please tell me you have the power to drug her."

Callum's eyes bored through Isobel, freezing her in place. The desire to pace fleeing under his gaze. All she could do was stare back at him. He looked devastatingly handsome in his black tux, which somehow made him seem even more manly and dangerous than usual.

"James Bond," Donna muttered, obviously seeing the same thing Isobel did.

"She doesn't need something to calm her down," Callum said. "She just needs to remember what she's doing and why she's doing it."

He strode across the room until he stood in front of her. His strong hand reached down to clasp her nape. "Hey darlin'," was all he said. But that deep rumbling brogue of his seeped right through her bones, providing a warm balm for her agitated soul as it did so.

Isobel couldn't speak. All she could do was stare up at the man she loved to distraction, willing him to understand something she didn't fully understand herself—the reason why she was freaking out.

His eyes scanned her face. "You love me," he said softly.

And her heart melted at the conviction in his words. A tear slipped down her cheek and his hand moved from her nape to cup her face, his thumb brushing away the tear.

"You want to be married to me." Again, it wasn't a question. He could see right into her soul and knew the truth.

She fell into his eyes. Losing herself in his strength and in the certainty that he loved her completely. That he would do anything for her. Including save her from herself.

"This isn't about the marriage," he said softly. "It's about the wedding."

His eyes left hers and scanned the room, taking in the discarded dress in Donna's hold, before returning to her. "I'll fix this. Trust me."

Isobel let out a sob and threw herself into his arms, feeling them wrap around her without a second's hesitation. She shivered in his hold, overwhelmed and needing his strength. His strong hands were gentle but firm on her back as he reassured her with his touch.

"Mairi," he said. "Call the vicar and get him over here. I don't care who else turns up. Donna, forget the dress. Pull out that blue one she wore on our date last month. Agnes, sort out the living room. We'll be down as soon as the vicar gets here."

And just like that, the room cleared of everyone except Donna, who began rooting around in the massive closet.

Isobel clung to Callum, breathing him in, drowning her fears in his unique scent that always reminded her of autumn in the highlands. Of perfect evening walks under the changing trees, listening to the water lap at the shores of the loch. He was her happy place. The only thing that made sense in her spiraling, chaotic mind.

"Nice underwear," he said with amusement in his voice. His hand stroked the curve of her behind, over the ivory lace that clung to it.

Isobel sniffed. "The corset's too tight." And stupid. She looked like a virgin on her wedding night. A girl trying too hard to seduce the man she'd married.

"Let's get it off you then." His voice deepened, and she shivered for an entirely different reason than panic.

The floor creaked as Donna approached. Isobel hid her face against Callum's chest, feeling the silk of his shirt against her burning cheek. She'd made a fool of herself. Again.

"Here's the dress and matching shoes. If you need help with anything else, sing out. I have my phone back."

"Thanks. Put them on the bed." Callum tightened his hold on Isobel, as though he knew embarrassment had set in.

The door closed behind Donna, and Isobel looked up at him. "I can't wear a sparkling blue dress to get married."

"Why not?" His eyes were dark and intense, telling her she was the only thing in his world at that moment.

Isobel blinked at him, her mind blank. "It's not the done thing," was all she could think of to say.

His chuckle was deep and sexy as hell. "Neither's getting married in the living room, but we're doing that in about twenty minutes. How about we get that dress on you before we go downstairs? Or, if you prefer, I can bring the vicar up here, and we can get married with you in your underwear."

Isobel gasped. "You wouldn't."

"Darlin' I'd do just about anything to make you my wife."

And just like that, with those words and the absolute honesty in his eyes, Isobel's fear and anxiety fled.

"Help me get dressed," she whispered.

"It will be my pleasure."

CALLUM McKAY WALKED HIS BRIDE DOWN THE STAIRS OF the old carriage house he'd converted behind his business in London's Chelsea district. The furniture had been pushed back to make room for their wedding guests, and they stood, beaming up at them.

Sophie ran around, a basket filled with rose petals in her hand, throwing them randomly at everyone and everything. Dressed in a tux, Jack stood at the bottom of the stairs, solemnly watching his mother descend.

"Don't worry," he said. "I have the rings."

"I wasn't worried," Callum told the teenager he was proud to call son. "I knew you'd make the perfect best man."

The boy ducked his head as his cheeks flushed, and Callum smiled, remembering well the age when he too had been teetering between boy and man, and everything had made him blush. Now, only one thing had the power to disarm him completely—his Isobel.

He looked down at the woman he loved, who had her hand tucked into his arm. She was perfection in the form-fitting, knee-length dress of midnight blue and shimmering sequins. It might not be a traditional wedding dress, but he couldn't imagine one more perfect for their day. The color made her green eyes sparkle and her creamy skin glow. And the dress brought back memories of the only other time she'd worn it and all the wonderfully wicked things he'd done to her.

As if reading his mind, she looked up at him, her eyes dark and knowing, her cheeks flushed.

"That really is a great dress," he said with heavy meaning.

"Stop it," she whispered. "My knees are weak enough."

"Don't worry; I'll hold you up."

"I know." The amount of love, the depth of it, in her eyes, made him want to carry her back upstairs and tell everyone to get the hell out of their house.

But he didn't.

He needed to tie this woman to him with everything he had, in case she realized she was far too good for him and ran away.

"Can we get on with it?" The vicar had been brought down from Invertary for the wedding at Betty insistence. Callum didn't even want to think about why Betty needed the old codger around for the after party. That sort of thinking made a man's balls shrivel and die.

Callum led Isobel over to stand in front of the ancient vicar.

"About bloody time," the man grumbled.

Callum looked down at Isobel. "You ready?"

"Yes." Her eyes sparkled. "I am completely ready to start the rest of my life with you."

A surge of pure possession tinged with relief rushed through him as he turned back to the vicar. "Keep it short and get on with it."

And, thankfully, the vicar did just that.

Kirsty and Lake Benson

Lake watched his wife from the shop window of his security store. His eyes ate her up as she walked across the cobbled street, the midday sun glinting in her long red hair. Today she wore a green pencil skirt that hugged her curves, a soft pink blouse that begged a man to touch, and a pair of pale pink stiletto heels. Damn, but he was almost drooling just from looking at her.

"I thought things cooled down once you'd been married for a few years," Ryan Granger, who was up from the London office for a meeting, commented from the door to the back of the shop. "You're looking at her like you're a starving man and she's a juicy steak."

"If things cool down in your marriage, you're doing something wrong. You might discover that for yourself one day." He cast a glance at the younger man. "Meeting's just been pushed back an hour."

"Yeah, I figured that." Ryan shook his head, as though Lake's behavior was a mystery to him. "Guess I'll go for a walk then."

"Text my receptionist and tell her to extend her lunch break, will you?"

"Sure." He dug his phone out of his pocket. "I'll let her know just how *busy* the boss is." With a wicked grin, he let himself out of the shop, saying hello to Kirsty as he passed.

"Where's he off to?" Kirsty said when she entered the store. "I thought you two had a meeting in a few minutes."

"We did, but I saw you coming this way and rescheduled." Lake reached behind his wife, turned the lock, and flipped the *Open* sign to *Closed*. "Now, I have a meeting with you."

"If you shut the shop, you'll lose customers," she joked.

They both knew the shop made a minuscule amount of money compared to Lake's security company. Two things stopped him from closing the shop for good—it kept him in touch with the community, and his wife's business was just across the street. Which meant *his wife* was just across the street. Something he very much enjoyed.

"I think I can afford to lose one or two sales," he said as he stepped closer to her.

"You do, do you?" She playfully backed away. "Do I need to remind you that we've got an expensive trip to the Amazon coming up?"

"No, but you might need to remind me why Joe and Julia decided it was a good place to celebrate their marriage."

He'd been to the Amazon. It was hot, humid, and full of stuff that could eat you. It wasn't his idea of the perfect honeymoon destination. But what did he know? He was just an ex-army boy trying to make a living doing what he loved— keeping people safe.

Taking his wife's hand, he gently tugged her toward the back of the building and the stairs that led up to his office.

"I don't have time for a *meeting*. I left Betty minding the shop because there was no one else to do it. If I don't get back there soon, she could burn the place to the ground. Or worse, redesign my summer collection."

"That's worse?"

"You've seen Betty's idea of fashion."

Lake chuckled as they reached the door to what had once been Kirsty's apartment. His business had quickly outgrown the space, and the rest of his Scottish team were now stationed in a building on the street behind the shop. But he'd never give up his office over the store. Not as long as Kirsty worked across from him.

"I only came over to tell you I'm booking our tickets to Peru and was wondering if you'd mind going via Miami. There's a lingerie fair that fits perfectly with our time frame. We could go to it on our way to the wedding."

"Sure," Lake said as he pushed his office door closed with his toe.

"It means three days of hanging around other lingerie designers and salespeople." She nibbled her bottom lip anxiously. "It won't be much fun for you."

Lake flicked the lock, securing them inside, away from prying eyes. "Will you be there?"

"Are you being deliberately dim? *I'm* the lingerie designer; it would be pretty pointless if you were there without me."

"If you're there, it will *definitely* be fun for me."

"Lake"—her eyes turned liquid—"you shouldn't say things like that unless you want me to get all mushy."

"I like you mushy." He liked her any way he could get her and suspected he would still feel the same way years from now. "You know what I was thinking this morning?"

"I'm afraid to ask."

"I was thinking about the first time I showed you my scars." He closed the distance between them, watching her pulse beat faster at the base of her throat. "This was your living room then." He shuffled them sideways a few inches.

"And we were standing about here when I stripped off to reassure you that you weren't the only one with scars. It's been a long time since then. We should do it again, just in case anything's changed."

Her emerald eyes sparkled up at him. "Didn't we *compare scars* before we came in to work this morning?"

"No, we were definitely comparing other things this morning." He grabbed his shirt and tugged it over his head before throwing it onto the desk beside him, enjoying the way his wife's eyes flared at the sight of his chest.

"Still so muscled." Her palms ran up the center of his chest, teasing the hair that grew there. "I remember wondering how often you had to work out to stay this way. I've always loved your chest hair. Only there's some gray in among the blond now." She looked up at him through thick lashes. "It's sexy."

"Glad you think so, because there's going to be a whole lot more gray over the next few years." Although, he *still* worked out every day to ensure his body was in prime condition to age well—and to keep that look in his wife's eyes.

"Mmm?" She wasn't listening. Both hands were massaging his pecs, and for a second, he thought she planned to lean forward and take a bite.

"Your scars are nothing more than silver lines now," he said as he traced the barely visible crisscrossed marks on her throat. His jaw clenched at the thought of her trapped in that car all those years ago, waiting to be rescued while her blood poured out.

A kiss to his jaw eased his tension. "That was a long time ago," she soothed him. "Now I have my very own warrior to watch over me."

"I'll always watch over you. That's my job. To keep you safe, so you don't have to worry about anything and can just enjoy life." He kissed her with slow, languorous touches until they were both breathing hard. "It's also my privilege."

"You were born in the wrong time." She ran her fingers through his short hair. "You should have been a knight."

"I think the role of King Arthur would have suited me better. I like being in charge." With a sweeping gesture, he slid her blouse from her shoulders and let it fall to the floor.

"Sneaky," she said with breathless admiration. "I didn't even feel you unbutton it."

"I'm a man of many skills." And then his words were stolen from him at the sight of her lingerie.

"You like?" Her voice broke through his daze.

"You weren't wearing this when you left the house this morning." The words came out as a hoarse croak.

She pushed her satin-covered breasts out toward him. "It's that new fifties-inspired line I've been working on. What do you think?"

"I'd need to see all of it to make an informed decision."

Her smile was pure seduction. "I can help with that."

Slowly, steadily, her eyes still on him, she unzipped her skirt, and let it slide down her body to pool on the floor. She stepped out of it, standing before him in matching lingerie, the exact same color as her shoes.

That's when he knew her visit to his shop had been more than an update on their travel plans—his wife wanted him. And didn't that just make him feel like he was already King Arthur? Adjusting himself in his jeans, he perched against the edge of his desk and made a circular motion for her to turn.

With a knowing smile, she made a slow pirouette, swaying her hips with each tiny step. The panties were high cut at her thighs but came up almost to her belly button; the bra band under the cups was several inches thick and sat just above her belly button. The bra didn't clasp at the back; instead, it fastened with several tiny pearl buttons. The band of the bra and its straps were made of a pale pink satin tartan. The cups were plain pink satin, and the panties were a mixture of both materials, with tartan panels over her hips. It covered more of her than most one-piece swimsuits. And was the sexiest thing he'd ever seen.

"Hell," he groaned.

"It's a longline bra and full coverage panty with a high leg," Kirsty said as she turned.

She might as well have been speaking Swedish because Lake didn't understand a word.

And he was through talking.

It seemed his wife wasn't though; she was still explaining her design, and experience told him that her enthusiasm could go on for quite a while. Something he planned to cut short for the moment. As soon as she'd fully turned to face him, his hands were on her waist, his mouth covering hers. Kirsty melted against him, her arms snaking lazily around his shoulders. He'd never get used to the sensation of her soft curves under his hands. Every day, she became more beautiful.

"I need you," she whispered between kisses.

"You can have me. Anytime you want."

"Now," she ordered as he cupped her satin-covered breasts.

"Now's good. Lose the panties but keep the bra and shoes."

With a moan, she pressed her breasts against his hold. Lake teased her throat with kisses as he backed up to the sofa. When his knees caught it, he released her, only to sit down and look up at her.

"Take the panties off," he ordered, "and come straddle me."

Keeping his eyes on hers, he undid his jeans and released his hard length from confinement.

"Bossy," she whispered, turning her back and wiggling her backside as she slipped the panties over her hips and down her thighs.

"Damn," he growled as he wrapped his fist around himself and stroked. Once, twice. He felt primed and ready to go, like a teenage boy with no control. "Don't think I'm going to last long," he confessed.

She turned back to him, her eyes sparkling as she slowly straddled him. "Guess that means this underwear will be a best seller."

"I'm already a fan." He held himself in position for her as he reached for her hip. "But it isn't the underwear that drives me crazy; it's you."

"Lake," she whispered.

"You ready for me?" he asked gruffly.

"Always."

With agonizing slowness, she lowered herself onto his length until their bodies were flush, and her soft, hot wetness engulfed him. She threw back her head and moaned with delight once they were joined.

"I love you," she wailed at the ceiling.

Lake broke into a rare smile as he leaned into her, tormenting her sensitive nipples with his teeth through the satin of her bra.

"You aren't moving," he teased.

Her nails dug into his shoulders, and each time he nipped at her, he could feel her internal muscles clench around him. At this rate, she wouldn't need to move. He'd blow anyway.

"Sit back," Kirsty said breathlessly.

With one last suck on her nipple, he did as he was told, his hands resting on her hips. She was a vision. A goddess looking down at him. Her russet colored hair wild around her shoulders, her milky skin flushed with pleasure, her lips swollen from his kisses.

"Still not moving." He smiled as he flexed his thighs, lifting his hips and thrusting into her.

"Oh…" Her eyes slowly closed as she rode the sensation.

He wished he could freeze the moment, to always see her like this. Her head thrown back with abandon, her skin flushed, her breaths coming in pants. They were completely vulnerable with each other, joined together, the way they were meant to be. Two halves of one whole.

There would never be another woman for him. There couldn't be. Even if he woke up tomorrow and Kirsty wasn't in his life, there wouldn't be a replacement. She was *it* for him. Only Kirsty. Always.

He reached up, clasped the back of her neck and brought her face down to his. Dark, sensually drowsy eyes gazed into him, and his heart clenched so tight he feared it would break.

"I love you," he told her softly. "More every day."

"Lake," she sighed, and then her lips were on his.

He held her tight, wrapping his arms around her as she made slow rhythmical movements with her hips that stroked his length deep inside of her and made all thoughts dissolve from his mind.

"My Lake," she whispered against his lips.

Yeah, he was hers, and only hers.

Forever.

Ryan's Heart

"I'm worried about you," Ryan's granddad said as they worked out together in the London office's basement training room. Well, Ryan was working out. He wasn't sure what the hell his granddad, Bill, and great-uncle, Bob, were doing.

"I'm fine," Ryan said as he pummeled the speed bag.

"You haven't been right since you came back from South America," Bob said as he stripped down to his white long johns and ill-fitting white vest.

Ryan frowned at the man as he neatly folded his work overalls and put them on the bench beside the wall. "You know there's a changing room, don't you? With lockers and everything."

"Doesn't feel right using the lockers," Bill said as he put his clothes beside his brother's. "We're only contractors, not part of the official team."

"But you feel fine about using the workout room any time the fancy takes you?" Ryan said.

They shared a look before Bob answered, "Well, yeah.

We're semi-permanent contractors. That's got to come with *some* perks."

Their twisted logic almost brought a smile to Ryan's face. Which would have been the first in months. The men weren't semi-permanent anything. They'd just been hired to do some joinery work months earlier and had never left. Since retiring years earlier, they'd only taken the jobs that interested them, and apparently, Benson Security was fascinating because they'd been inventing reasons to hang around ever since they first walked through the door.

Of course, the fact they could hassle him while they were there was also one of their perks.

"He's right, you know," Bob said as he started his warm-up, which involved swinging his arms around aimlessly. "You haven't been the same since you got back. You don't smile so much."

"Still eat a helluva lot though," his granddad said with a grin.

That was true, but now every calorie he took into his body was turned into pure muscle. He'd bulked up quite a bit since the South American operation, gaining strength but losing none of his agility. Getting in peak form had taken a lot of hard work. It had also given him an excuse to come down to the basement and punch things whenever the need arose. Which was frequently. Mainly because he was mad that he'd been played for a fool by some woman he'd met in Peru.

He was tired of being seen as the team fool. Tired of being known for how much food he consumed and how much time he spent playing on his Xbox. He was just as well-trained as every other member of his team. More so than some. Megan had never spent time in the army. She hadn't spent years taking on terrorists in Afghanistan. He was a professional, damn it. So what if he had crap taste in women and was easily suckered in by a pretty face? He sure as hell wasn't going to be that gullible again.

"See what I mean?" His granddad's words penetrated his thoughts. "He's been full of anger since that trip. Always punching something."

"Son," Bob said. "You need to talk to somebody." When Ryan glanced over at him, he threw up his hands. "Not me! Somebody else."

"Not me either," Bill said. "How about your grandmother? If you catch her on a night when she isn't going to bingo, she'll have plenty of time to listen. But not before *Coronation Street*. She'll cut you off like you're dead to her if that comes on the telly while you're talking."

"I'm not talking to Gran." He steadied the speed bag and turned to the heavy bag. Talking to his family always brought on the urge to punch something, and hard. "I don't need to talk to anybody. There's nothing wrong."

"There's nothing wrong?" Bob said, two sets of overly hairy eyebrows shooting up as they both stared at him.

"Son," his granddad said, "you're spending so much time hitting things, you're beginning to look like the termite man."

Ryan stopped mid-punch and stared at the two tiny gnome-like men in their long underwear. "Termite man?"

"You know the guy," Bill said. "From the movies. Keeps saying 'I'll be back.'" He looked at his brother. "To be fair, he does always come back."

"Man of his word." Bob nodded. "Got to respect that."

"And hard to kill."

"Because of all the steroids."

"Got to use steroids to get muscles like that," Bill agreed before looking back at Ryan. "You're not taking steroids, are you? They cause impotence." He patted his ample belly. "I'd rather lose the muscle and keep the ability to please your grandmother."

"I'm going to puke," Ryan said. "And it's the Terminator. As in, he puts an end to things. He's got nothing to do with bugs."

"Makes sense." Bill nodded before lifting a staff from the wall of practice weapons. "You ready?" he asked his brother.

"Just let me get my stick."

Rolling his eyes, Ryan returned to punching the bag, but a movement out of the corner of his eye distracted him again. He turned to see his granddad and great-uncle circling each other, in what could only be described as slow motion. Now and then, they'd smack their sticks together like a couple of half-dressed, rhythmless Morris dancers. It was the most bizarre thing he'd seen in a long time. And that was saying a lot because he'd spent time living in Invertary.

"Is there a reason you two feel you need to work out in your underwear?" Ryan said.

"Why buy something new when this works fine?" Bob said as he tapped Bill's stick with his. "Nearly got me there," he said. "We're definitely improving."

"If the building's attacked again, we'll be ready this time."

"It helps that we have the panic room now."

"Just in case we panic. Which reminds me, there's nothing like a good glass of gin when you feel panicked. We need to stock up that room."

"Already done," Bob said.

It was no use. It was impossible to work out with the two of them in the room, playing with sticks and talking rubbish. He watched them as he unwrapped the tape from his hands. It was like watching those two hobbit cousins of Frodo attempting to fight. He looked down at their slowly dancing feet. Wouldn't you know it? They were hairy.

As he watched, they stopped circling each other and stood, panting.

"Never been so fit in my life as since I came to work here," Bill said.

Bob patted his rounded middle. "I ran up the stairs the other day, and I wasn't even out of breath."

"Kill me now," Ryan muttered, making a mental note to talk to Callum about rescinding his family's building access. Coming to work would be a whole lot more pleasant if he wasn't being followed around by two geriatric gnomes who confused age with wisdom.

"You know," Bill said. "It happened to me once too. And if you tell your grandmother this, I'll swear you're a liar."

He knew he shouldn't ask. That was how they sucked you in. One innocent statement that made no bloody sense. The next thing you knew, you were asking for an explanation, and then, that was you. Sucked down the rabbit hole that was the Granger brothers' brains.

But, even knowing that, he couldn't stop the question coming out of his mouth. "What happened?" he said between gritted teeth.

"Got screwed by a woman," Bill said, gazing off into the distance. "And I mean that in every sense of the word. Gladys was the prettiest little thing you ever did see. Big blue eyes and a smile so innocent all you wanted to do was hold her in your arms and shelter her from the world. I took her to bed, as you do. Woke up the next morning with no wallet and my best boots missing." He grinned at his brother. "It was worth every penny." He cleared his throat. "I mean, that's what I think now. Back then, I fancied myself in love and being conned like that devastated me."

"It's not the same thing," Ryan said. Although it was a little too close for comfort.

"I tracked her down you know." Bill sounded wistful.

Bob's staff dropped to the mat with a dull thud. "You did?"

His granddad nodded. "Few years later. She was working

as a lady of the night. Broke my heart to see it. But I think she'd been in that line of work all along. Only, now she was up-front about it. If you know what I mean."

"How did the meeting go?"

"Cost me ten bob." The grin was wide.

"You didn't?" his brother said, and then they held on to each other as they fell about laughing.

With a shake of his head, Ryan picked up his towel and water bottle. "Thanks for the pep talk. It was something else. As usual."

"My point is," Bill said when he'd stopped laughing, "we all get taken for a ride sometimes, son. Not every woman's like that, but some are. You need to kiss a lot of frogs to find your princess."

"I'm not looking for a princess," Ryan said. "I'm perfectly happy on my own. Women are too much trouble." He'd learned that lesson the hard way, at the expense of his reputation with his team. These men and women expected him to have their backs. Not to get distracted by his dick with every passing woman.

Bob looked sad. "She might have had a good reason for what she did," he said.

Ryan strode past them toward the changing room and the showers. "There's always a good reason—for them. It's never good for me. Don't worry about me, Pops. I'm good. She used me and I let my team down. It won't happen again."

As he heard the door close behind him, his granddad's soft voice came to him. "Oh, I hope it does, son. Because the alternative is no life at all."

With that, Ryan headed to the showers.

Harry and Magenta

Harry Boyle's mind was on other things as he dodged through the crowds in Addis Mercato, the biggest market in Africa. He was surrounded by people, animals, and vehicles. There were folk buying spices from stalls with perfect cone-shaped piles of powder on them. They'd scoop some spice into a little bag for their customer, then spend their time making the cone smooth again as they waited for another sale. A donkey carrying a pile of over-stuffed bags wandered past a table where women haggled over lengths of brightly colored cloth.

He dodged around a display of intricately woven baskets being sold from a blanket on the ground, and barely missed toppling a woman who held a pole laden with *jebenas*—the local clay formed coffee pots. From plastic containers to shoes made of recycled tires, the market had everything you could ever need and a lot of things you wouldn't.

But, on that hot, dry morning, where the red dust rose from the earth to coat your feet, Harry didn't pay attention to the chaos around him. His eyes were fixed firmly on his feet as his brain raced over the lines of code he needed to perfect for the British government. This was why, when a man with a pile of overfilled bags balanced on top of his head stepped into his path—Harry walked into him. The bags fell to the ground, Harry tripped over them and landed flat on his back in the dirt.

And a nearby donkey sat on his legs.

There was a second when it felt like the whole world paused to look at the white man trapped under the ass of a donkey. And then, the world laughed.

"Harry!"

He groaned and shut his eyes as he heard his wife rush through the crowd to get to him. Unlike Harry, who blended into the woodwork, people tended to notice Magenta. He wasn't sure if it was the Goth effect of her black makeup and clothes, or just because Magenta wouldn't tolerate anyone getting in her way.

"Help me get that donkey off him," she snapped. "Harry, are you okay?"

He opened an eye and saw her face above his, the bright blue of the sky framing her black hair like a halo. "The internet's down," he said. "Well, not all of it. Just our hotel's connection. I was heading to the Hilton to use their Wi-Fi."

The weight of the donkey lifted from him, and the beast brayed loudly in complaint. Apparently, Harry made a comfortable seat.

"Come on," Magenta said. "Get up before someone trips over you."

She reached out her hand and helped Harry to his feet. He gamely smiled back at his grinning audience as his wife patted the dust off his back. Today she wore black denim cut-off shorts, a black vest-top, and black canvas Converse. Several strings of black and white ceramic beads that she'd bought in Nigeria were wrapped around her wrist. She'd tied her dyed black hair up in a high ponytail, and this softened the effect of the thick black eyeliner framing her eyes. As usual, she was stunning.

He knew he was grinning at her like a loon, but he couldn't help it. His whole life, all he'd wanted was to be with Magenta. Ever since he'd seen her in the playground when they were tiny. Now, he got to be with her every day.

"What am I going to do with you?" she said when she saw the grin.

"I can think of a few things. But maybe we shouldn't do any of them in public."

She took his hand. "Yeah, in public is definitely out." She started walking, pulling him along with her.

"Where are we going?" Harry said.

"To the hotel. To find the internet you need."

He could feel the burn in his cheeks. Thirty years old, and he still embarrassed himself at every turn. It was a good job he was smart; otherwise, his ego would have been dust by now.

"I've figured out the kink in that code I'm working on for the Department of Defence. I just need to get it to them, and they can run a diagnostic." The work he did for the UK government was top secret, but he loved the challenge it provided.

After he'd sold his security program to the government for a mint, he'd tried to go into semi-retirement and focus on setting up a literacy charity with his dyslexic wife, but coding kept calling to him. There was nothing like the challenge of writing code. Of pitting your brain against the world's best hackers and seeing who came out on top. Apart from sex with Magenta, it was the best high he could think of.

"I've lost you again, haven't I?" Magenta tugged at his hand and smiled up at him.

"Were you talking?" He often zoned out when his brain

was niggling away at a problem. His wife had become used to it.

"I was saying that we've almost set up the school now. We hired the last staff member this morning."

"That's great." He wanted to sweep her up and hug her tight to show his admiration. But the middle of a bustling market wasn't the best place. A thought struck him, and his stomach fell. "I was supposed to be at that interview, wasn't I?"

They turned up a dusty street with shanty style houses on one side of the road and high-rise buildings on the other— one of them, the hotel Harry had been aiming for. It always disturbed him that a luxury hotel overlooked the tin roofs of the shanty. It made him feel enormously guilty that he had so much when so many had so little.

"We're doing what we can to help," Magenta said, as though reading his mind.

"I know." It was the reason they'd set up a charity to run schools in some of the poorest parts of the world to help educate kids who couldn't afford it. And all of it was paid for with the money he'd made from selling his security software to the government. Which reminded him, he really must tweak some of his notes before he sent them off to his colleagues...

"And he's off again." Magenta grinned at him.

"I'm sorry." He wrapped an arm around her shoulders and pulled her into his side as her arm snaked around his waist. "I'll get this done, then we can have dinner, and I promise to concentrate on every word you say."

"I know you will." She gave him a squeeze. "Go do what you need to do and meet me in the lobby bar. And, if you get lost in your work and don't appear within the next couple of hours, I'll come find you."

His shoulders sagged with relief. Him getting lost in his

work was a distinct possibility. "See you soon." He pressed a quick kiss to her lips and headed for the business center.

⁂

MAGENTA DIDN'T HAVE TO TRACK HER HUSBAND DOWN. HE managed to find his way to the Hilton lobby bar less than an hour after he'd gone in search of an internet connection.

There were dark circles under his eyes from too many nights spent working on his code, because his days had been filled helping her run their charity. He absentmindedly pushed his hair from his forehead as he smiled at her, and, as usual, her heart flipped at the sight. Harry's genius IQ meant that when he focused on something, it got *all* of his attention. He honestly didn't see anything but the object of his focus. And when that object was her, the feeling was indescribable. There was nothing in the world like having all of Harry's attention.

He flopped his long, lean body into the chair beside her and eyed the tablet in her hand. "School stuff?"

"Tightening loose ends for the new board of trustees." She put the tablet aside. "How did it go? Get the code sent okay?"

"Yeah, but the internet here's even slower than our hotel's connection." He signaled for the waiter, who headed their way. "Have you ordered already?"

"No, I was waiting for you."

They gave their choices to the waiter and relaxed back into their leather seats. The crisp, clean marble-and-metal décor of the bar was in stark contrast to the dusty chaos outside the door of the hotel. Gentle background music played as cool air pumped through the room. They could have been in a hotel anywhere in the world. There was nothing around them to indicate that they were in the middle of Ethiopia.

Magenta leaned across the table and took her husband's hand in hers. "You're fed up with all the traveling, aren't you?"

He jerked at her comment, his hand tightening on hers. "I don't mind it. I only want you to be happy."

And there it was, the reason her love for Harry often overwhelmed her. "I am happy. You make me that way."

"Then we're good." And he meant it. As far as he was concerned, the topic was closed.

Harry would bend over backward to give her everything she wanted, even if it meant sacrificing some of the things he needed. It was her job to make sure his needs were fulfilled too. One she'd slacked on these past couple of years, mainly because she'd been so busy setting up their schools. But it was time that changed.

"I want to make you happy too," she said.

"You do." He leaned across the table, eager to reassure her.

Magenta shook her head to stop whatever he was about to say. "You're getting antsy. I see it. You want to be working again."

"I do work. I work on the charity with you, and I do the odd job with Benson Security. Then there's the government work."

"Which you can't do properly, because we're always moving, and the internet connections are spotty at best. Plus, you're limited in what you can do because you need a secure connection. You're doing half the job you want to do, and it's obvious you're getting frustrated."

"It's working out okay. I don't have any complaints."

No, he wouldn't. Because that wasn't how he functioned. It was time she complained on his behalf. Even if it meant the complaint was against herself. "The charity isn't your thing," she said softly. "I know you're supporting me in it, but it isn't your first love. Coding is. I've been selfish making you focus on the schools these past few years."

"Don't be daft. You haven't been selfish. And you're wrong about my first love. It's you, baby. Always has been, always will be."

And that's why things had to change. Harry would never look out for himself; he'd always put her first. It was time she did the same for him. "The Benson Security work isn't stretching you either. You could do it in your sleep. Let's face it, you don't have a whole lot of interest in the company. You mainly went into partnership with Lake and Callum to help them out." She gentled her voice. "They don't need you now. They've established their reputation, and they have Elle to do their computer stuff. I think it's time you cut your ties with the business."

Harry started to protest, but his shoulders relaxed some. Which was a dead giveaway that the idea appealed to him.

"Honey," Magenta said to stop his protest. "I think it's time we moved back to Scotland."

His gaze shot to hers, and he focused in on her, the way only Harry could: not missing one tiny thing. "You mean it?"

She nodded. "I've been thinking about it a lot these past few months. The charity is well established now, and there are a lot of skilled people in Africa who are far more knowl-edgeable about setting up a school than I'll ever be. I'm self-aware enough to realize that working with the charity these past few years has been more about helping me deal with growing up dyslexic than it ever was about running the schools." She knew her smile was rueful. "I think we should employ an African team to move around and set things up, then let them get on with it."

"No." Harry leaned in, ready to argue her case even against herself.

"You know it's true," she cut him off. "Finding out at

twenty-one that I wasn't dumb, that I just had a learning issue, rocked my world. Having you, and the bags of cash you don't care about has made it easy to throw myself into setting up something to ensure other kids don't have to suffer what I did." She reached for his other hand, holding them both tight, as she stared into the eyes of the man she loved more than she loved breathing. "You're an amazing man. Your support over the past few years has changed everything about my life and given me confidence in *me*. It's time I gave something back to you."

"You give me everything, baby. There's nothing else to give."

Damn, but she loved her man. "I want to move back to Scotland. I want to run my own caving company like I always planned. And I want you to have great internet access, lots of computery gadgets, and your brother close enough to watch football with on a Saturday. I want to go home to Invertary."

His lips quirked. "Not sure computery is a technical term."

"We'll make it one. What do you say, Hairy Boil? Want to go home to Invertary with me once we've sorted this school?"

His goofy smile made her heart beat faster. "Yeah, Maggie Fraser-*Boil*, I do."

"Good. Then while I sort out the last few loose ends to get the school up and running, you need to ring Lake and sell your share in the business to him. Agreed?"

"Yeah, agreed. But you know we can still travel to check on the schools, right?"

"I know." She leaned across the table and kissed her husband, long and hard.

The sound of a throat being cleared brought them up for air, and they turned to find their waiter grinning down at them. "Do you want these meals to take to your room?" he asked.

"This isn't actually our hotel," Harry told him.

The smile grew wider. "Do you want me to get you a room?"

"No," Magenta said. "I think we're good." Then she looked at her husband. "But eat fast, yeah?"

"Oh, yeah," he agreed with that sparkle in his eyes that she loved.

A London Night

Elle Roberts stepped out of her favorite Mexican restaurant in the heart of Soho and breathed in the unique fragrance of a London summer. As usual, the theater district was packed with people. The many restaurants overflowed with chattering patrons, and the scent of different cuisines battled for supremacy in the warm night air. A person could get lost in the crowds of Soho. Elle had spent years doing just that.

"Do you want us to walk you to the Underground?" Megan said as she came out of the doors behind Elle.

"No, I'm fine."

"A woman shouldn't walk alone in the dark in London," Dimitri said as he threw an arm around Megan's shoulders.

"Ignore him," Megan said. "He's almost as much of a Neanderthal as my brother-in-law."

"I'm not a Neanderthal. I'm using common sense. I've seen Elle during self-defense training, and it ain't pretty. She's the most helpless member of our team. Hell, baby, she can't even fire a gun."

Megan rolled her eyes at Elle. "Bet that makes you feel so

much better. Anyway, she doesn't need a gun. She can hit an attacker over the head with her laptop."

That made Dimitri groan. He'd teased her all evening about bringing her laptop out to dinner with them. Elle had calmly informed him that her laptop was her date—if only that weren't so close to the mark.

"You two go see your show." They were off to watch a risqué late-night cabaret in the heart of Soho. "I'll take myself home. Trust me, I'm fine. I walk alone all the time. And look around you, there are more people here than there usually are on the streets when I walk home after work."

"I don't like that either. I'm going to talk to the guys. We need to set up a schedule of people to escort you home when you work late." Dimitri frowned, and Elle knew he was seconds away from insisting they act as her bodyguards until she got to the subway.

"Megan," Elle said on a sigh. "Can you deal with him, please?"

"Don't worry. I've got this." With wide blue eyes and a loving smile, her blonde friend gazed up at the man she adored. "Come with me now, or I will shoot you somewhere painful but non-essential."

His eyebrows shot up his forehead. "You have a gun on you?"

She shrugged. "You don't?"

Dimitri looked like his head was going to explode, and that was Elle's cue to make a getaway. It seemed that even though Megan was now an official security team member instead of a trainee, Dimitri still thought he was the boss of their partnership. Elle was pretty sure Megan never got the memo about the hierarchy.

"I'm leaving now. Have a great time at the show." She gave them a cheerful wave and walked away as their raised voices wafted after her. They were too busy arguing to even notice she'd gone.

The evening showing of *Harry Potter* had just ended, and the Palace Theatre crowd streamed out into the street in front of her. Their excited chatter made her grin as she cut through them on her way to Chinatown. The nearest Underground station was a straight walk down Charing Cross Road, but Elle wasn't in the mood to go home to an empty flat. She wanted to wander, hang out with the crowds and spend an hour feeling like she was part of something bigger than herself.

In front of her, a large group of tourists stopped to stare up at the buildings, blocking her path. With a shake of her head, Elle skirted around them. As she passed a small side alley, an arm snaked around her waist from behind, and a hand clamped over her mouth. Strong arms held her tight as she was rushed into the dark, narrow alley. She was being abducted. In the middle of London. Surrounded by people who didn't even notice. Shock froze her for a beat, and then adrenaline kicked in.

But before she could strike out, she felt her attacker's mouth close to her ear. "Did you miss me, gorgeous?"

David.

She slumped against him. And then she got furious. What the hell was he doing? Trying to scare her to death?

She kicked back at him and had the satisfaction of feeling her heel hit his shin. She was planning her next move when suddenly she was turned and pressed against the wall. The tall, lean, muscled body of the man she obsessed over leaned into her until he was flush against her softness.

"I should knee you in the balls for almost giving me a heart attack," she told him.

"Ellie, we both know that's the last thing you want to do with that part of my anatomy."

His brown hair was longer than the last time she'd seen him, several months earlier in Scotland. Which reminded her. "You left me handcuffed to a bed! With pink fluffy cuffs!"

His smile made her internal organs liquify and pool low in her body.

"I told you to stop searching for me, but you didn't listen, did you?"

"I thought it was more of a suggestion than an order." Not that she would have obeyed any order he gave, anyway.

"You've stirred up a hornet's nest, Ellie." A flash of cold steel appeared in his eyes before disappearing, and he went back to looking at her with warmth. "I'm going to tell you again, and this time it is an order." He paused as he twirled some of her shoulder-length pale blue hair around his finger. "Stop searching for information about my identity. If you don't, you're going to bring down a heap of trouble on your head, and the heads of your friends and workmates."

His tone was soft and seductive, completely at odds with his harsh words. But there was also something else in there. Something he wasn't saying. Something that set alarm bells ringing.

"Are you okay?" she asked.

His eyes softened. "I can take care of myself."

That didn't answer her question, and all that heat pooling low in her stomach suddenly felt like concrete starting to set. "I've caused trouble for you." And she suspected it was the kind of trouble they couldn't laugh about. Suddenly, her search for him seemed far more serious than she'd thought it would be, and for the first time since starting it, she wondered exactly what kind of mess she was digging into.

For a micro-second, his jaw clenched before it relaxed again. But the small tell gave her all the information she needed. He was in danger. Because of her.

She flattened her palm against his chest, over the soft

thudding of his heart, and felt his heat sear her fingers. "Benson Security can help you."

"I don't need any help. Everything is fine."

"Do you have to lie to me?"

"Ellie, you think I'm a spy. Why would you expect me to tell the truth?"

He had a point. "I won't search for you anymore, on one condition."

"I like how you think you can negotiate with me. It's cute."

Elle rolled her eyes. They both knew she would eventually dig up every piece of information there was on him. It was just a matter of time. "If you promise to contact Benson Security, and let us help you if things get too hot to handle, I'll stop searching."

He leaned forward, pressing their bodies together until all she could feel was his heat at her front and the cool hard wall at her back. His nose trailed up her throat until his lips were at her ear. "Your logic is off, Ellie. You know I'm a liar, so why would you believe any promise I made?"

Elle wasn't sure why she knew he'd keep his word to her, maybe it was just wishful thinking, but she was certain he would. "Give me your word."

"Fine." He breathed out over the shell of her ear, making her shiver. "You have my word. *If* I need help, I'll contact Benson Security."

"You'll contact me." She wanted to make that clear.

He tugged at her earlobe with his teeth. "I'll contact you," he whispered.

And somehow his words felt like a promise to do far more than simply get in touch.

"Then I'll stop searching." At least she would try, because he was her obsession now, and it wouldn't be easy to quit doing something that consumed her.

"Tell me something," he said as he leaned back to look at her. "Do you still dream about me?"

"That night was an anomaly." As was every single night since. The man invaded her dreams, each one hotter than the last. She burned for him now. And there wasn't a damn thing she could do about it. Not unless he decided to stop running from her, because she was convinced that was exactly what he was doing.

"So, you still dream about me." He sounded entirely too smug for her liking, but before she could tell him he was fooling himself, he kept talking. "I like this color." He stroked her hair. "It goes with your eyes. I like this pink dress too. You look like a fifties pin-up girl. A glamorous housewife. You should be in a kitchen somewhere, with a lace-edged apron, baking cookies for an army of kids before your husband comes home and sweeps you off your feet."

"Interesting fantasy you have there." Elle's eyes strayed to his lips as she remembered the kiss they'd shared, the same night he'd cuffed her to the bed. "A tad sexist and archaic for me though."

"Really?" His eyebrow cocked, and his smile stole the air from her lungs. "You don't like role play? I'll have to change your mind on that."

Yes, please! She blinked at him. "How about you play the stay-at-home husband? You can bake me some cookies, and when I'm done working, I'll sweep you off your feet."

He closed the distance between them until his lips were a hair's breadth from hers. "That works for me too."

"You drive me crazy," she whispered.

"Oh, you have no idea just how crazy I could make you." And then his lips were on hers.

The kiss was slow and sensual, stealing her sense of self-preservation with each delicious taste of him. She curled her fingers into his black tee and held on while her world spun out of control. This was what she remembered, what she dreamed about, what she longed for. When he slowly pulled away from her, her lips chased after his until she stood on tiptoe before him.

"Later, beautiful girl." He swept her hair from her face. "That is a promise."

And then he was gone, moving fast, blending into the night as he was swallowed up by the crowd. Leaving Elle, dazed and alone in the alley. With a trembling hand, she pressed her fingers to her lips. Who knew what trouble he was in, or when she'd see him again. And now, she didn't even have her searches for him to keep her occupied until his return. *If* he returned this time. Because every instinct she had screamed to her that he was in way more trouble than he'd let on. Stubborn, infuriating man-of-mystery. Too damned macho to ask for help.

With a huff of irritation, she yanked her bag onto her shoulder, then stilled.

Her laptop!

He'd stolen her life.

Her eyes narrowed as she stared into the darkness where he'd vanished. How could he? This was the ultimate betrayal. One for which he would pay. As far as she was concerned, their tenuous deal was off. There was no way she'd stop searching for him now.

Invertary's Unofficial Council Has a Plan

Dougal Jamieson, Invertary's unofficial mayor (unofficial because nobody had turned up to vote at the last eight elections) banged his gavel on the lectern for silence.

He didn't get it. Which came as no surprise. Town meetings were raucous at the best of times, but this one had attracted more attention than most—because the one and only point on their agenda had been penciled in as *Deal with the Betty situation*.

"Settle down," he boomed through the microphone, making his voice reverberate around the Presbyterian church hall.

Only half the people paid any attention to him. The rest were too busy gossiping about the subject of the meeting, who sat in the front row with a sly grin on her craggy old face. As usual, she'd dressed in a shapeless tartan dress and the smell of hot Scotch pies wafted from her black handbag. It was a relief to see that she'd stopped dyeing her head blue. Her head, not her hair because there wasn't enough of that left to dye. And, miracle of miracles, she actually had her teeth in for a change.

"I need silence," he bellowed and, at last, the noise petered out to nothing. "About time," he snapped at his fellow towns-folk. "Thank you for coming out on this cold night to attend our meeting. We"—he pointed at the council who sat in a row behind him, facing the crowd—"expect you to conduct your-selves in a civilized manner. There will be time for questions and comments later. *After* we've presented the issue to all of you. In the meantime, I'll introduce the council."

He turned to the people behind him. "Caroline McInnes, of course, needs no introduction, but I'll give her one anyway. She's married to Josh, lives in the castle, and runs everything. And I mean everything! She's been running this town for years. And recently, she's gone into business with Mitch Harris and is now managing the careers of some very talented musicians." He paused for effect. "And Josh."

As the crowd laughed and Josh complained loudly from the front row, Dougal moved on. "As you may be aware, both the principal of the high school and the minister of this church have retired. So we had two vacancies on the council. Reverend David Carlyle kindly filled one of them." When the younger man smiled at the crowd and a few cheeky women wolf-whistled, he just shook his head. The poor man had only been in Invertary a few weeks and was already being hounded by every available woman in the Highlands, all of them agreeing he was far too pretty to be living alone in the manse.

Clearing his throat, Dougal moved on to the additional two council members—because they'd had to expand to fill the town's growing needs. "This is Fiona Hendry, some of you might know her if you have kids in school. She's the new head teacher at the high school." *And too brand new to dodge taking on the old principal's place on the council.*

"And last but not least, you all know Lachlan McBride. We thought his engineering expertise might come in handy."

"And Lachlan thought he was only here to offer advice; he didn't realize he'd been conscripted onto the council," Lachlan drawled, making his three brothers at the back of the room laugh loudly and point at him.

"Aye, well, thanks for being here." Dougal moved swiftly on, turning back to the lectern. Placing his hands either side, he leaned into the mic. "As you know, the town is expanding."

"Mainly with Americans," Matt Donaldson, the town's only cop, called out. "It's an invasion."

"Hey." His American wife, Jena, smacked him on the chest. "Any more of that and I'll go back to the States. Then what would you do? The house still needs work, and you're garbage at DIY."

"You know I don't mean you, Princess," Matt said. "I was talking about Josh. He can go back any time." He grinned over at the singer, who flipped him off.

"None of that," Dougal snapped. "There are children present.

"Some of them yours," Caroline, Josh's wife, pointed out from behind Dougal, as their toddler sat at his side.

"Sorry, baby." Josh batted his eyelashes at her, making everyone laugh.

"Anyway, as I was saying." Keeping the town meetings on track was a herculean task. "The town is growing. Not a lot, but enough to make us think about the future. If we're going to keep the young people here and not lose their skills and enthusiasm to the big cities, then we need to generate more employment opportunities for them."

"Aye, aye," someone shouted.

"Couldn't agree more," someone added.

He held up his hands for silence. "With that in mind, a few of us have come up with some ideas for attracting business and investment to Invertary." He glanced at Betty, who looked more evil with every word he said. "I want to buy the empty building and carpark next to the Scottie Dog and build a conference center, which should attract people to the area. Someone else wants to set up a summer camp for kids, but the facilities could be used year-round for retreats. Magenta plans to come back at some point and open a caving business to take tourists into the old mine. We need more accommodation for all the looky-loos that turn up hoping to get a glimpse of Josh's ugly mug. We want to make the fishing competition and the lingerie fashion show regular events. Not to mention, expand our Christmas market. And there are a few other things in the works that we don't have time to talk about here."

He took a deep breath and eyed Betty. "I'm sure you'll all agree that's a lot of fine plans. Plans that will expand the town without ruining everything good about it. We just have one wee problem."

The loud cackle from the front row set his teeth on edge.

"It would seem," he said, "that a good portion of the properties we need to buy to make these business ideas a reality belong to Betty McLeod."

Betty let out a whoop as a ripple of shock ran around the room. Dougal well understood the reaction. He'd been stunned too when his lawyers had finally managed to dig through all the paperwork hiding the ownership of the mysterious trust that owned half of Invertary.

"Quieten down," he said into the microphone.

Margaret Campbell, owner of the local craft shop and leader of Knit or Die, shot to her feet. One look at her, and it was clear where her ex-model daughter, Kirsty, got her fine looks from. She was a gorgeous woman, and she was also enraged.

"How is this possible?" she said. "She ran a knicker emporium for about a million years. Where did she get the money to buy up Invertary? Are you sure this isn't one of her sick pranks? That she didn't just pay someone to fake ownership? Does she really own anything at all?"

"I'm sure," Dougal said. "Because we double-checked everything." He motioned to Lake, owner of Benson Security. "Your son-in-law investigated the whole thing for the council."

Lake, who sat beside Betty, gave his mother-in-law a sympathetic nod. "It's true. She really does own half the town."

And Betty cackled some more. Having the time of her life, as usual. How Lake Benson and Jodie Miller-Harris could stand being around the woman for any length of time was a mystery to everyone who lived in Invertary. The only explanation anyone had come up with that made any sense was that they were both English and, therefore, didn't know any better.

"How did you do it?" Margaret demanded of Betty. "Who did you steal from?"

"Nobody." The old woman grinned. "I'm just smarter than everybody in this room, and more besides." And then she was laughing again.

"As you can probably guess," Dougal said as he glared at Betty. "The problem isn't that Betty owns half of the town, it's that she won't sell to the rest of us."

The outrage was loud, and Betty seemed to feed off it, preening as though she were center stage at the Oscars. As everyone watched, she launched herself off her chair and waddled to the podium.

"Out of my way," she told Dougal with a shove.

Dougal stepped aside while he prayed for the strength not to murder the woman in front of him. She reached for the microphone and angled it down so she could speak into it.

"It's true," she said. "I own all the empty real estate in this town and some of the stuff you lot pay rent on."

"Holy crap," someone shouted. "I need to check my rental agreement. What's the name of the trust that manages the properties for her?"

"Tartan Terror Inc.," Betty announced.

A wail went up from another part of the room. "I've been paying my bakery's rent to Satan," Morag McKay cried.

At that, Betty laughed hard. "Aye, and it's going to go up an' all. You're skimping on the meat in your pies, and I've had enough of it."

More outraged shouting broke out around the room.

"How can she be wealthy and dress in tartan rubbish bags?" Jean demanded.

"Why has she waited this long to tell us she owns the place?" Shona shouted.

"Because," Betty said through the sound system, "unlike the rest of you, I know how to play the long game. I knew that one day, you were going to wise up to the potential of our wee town, and I would be there to cash in on it. It's amazing what selling knickers will net you. While you were buying fancy dresses to woo the likes of this idiot here"—she cocked a thumb at Dougal, who turned red at the memory of his short dalliance with Jean—"I was buying property when it was dirt cheap, because nobody else wanted it." Her grin was pure evil. "Well, look who wants it now." And then she started laughing again.

"Lake," Dougal called to one of the only people in the room who could corral Betty.

With a shake of his head, the Englishman dragged a chair over beside the lectern and put Betty on it. He stood beside her, his feet apart and his arms folded, while Dougal returned to the mic. It was unclear whether Lake's stance was an attempt to protect Betty from the angry mob or to protect everyone else from Betty.

"Settle down," Dougal called, but no one listened. He banged his gavel several times as he shouted, "I said, settle down!"

There was reluctant settling.

"Okay, so here's the thing. Betty has said she's open to negotiation over the properties in her portfolio." And didn't that sentence just stick in the throat? "Unfortunately, being Betty, she doesn't only want to negotiate with the prospective buyers. She wants to negotiate with the whole town. Apparently, there are a few things she'd like to happen before she considers selling. Things she needs to..." He gave her a look of disgust before forming air quotes around what he had to say next, *"put her in the mood."*

The loud groans were very much heartfelt by everyone in the room.

"I made a list," Betty announced, before digging into her handbag.

She came out with a piece of paper covered in tomato sauce stains. At least, Dougal hoped they were sauce and not the blood of some other poor sucker she'd tortured to death with her sense of humor.

"Microphone," she snapped at Dougal, as though he were her servant.

For a second, his head felt like it might explode, then he remembered she had him over a barrel if he wanted to build his conference center, and he was pretty sure steam came out of his ears.

Lake cocked an eyebrow at Dougal, took the mic, and gave it to Betty. "Don't let her get to you," he said. "She loves it."

Betty ignored them both, too busy focusing on her list.

"Number one," she said, her voice reverberating around the room and making people cringe. "I want to be called Empress Betty by everyone in town." There were loud groans. "I considered Queen Betty, but that sounds like a drag act, and England already has a Queen Betty."

"This is hell," Josh said to anyone who would listen.

He wasn't wrong.

"Number two," Betty carried on like she wasn't aware of the chaos she was causing with every word out of her mouth. "I want free pies for life from Morag's bakery."

Morag shot to her feet, followed closely by her two cronies, who belonged to her morality society. "I am not giving you free anything." As she spoke, she stretched out an arm and pointed at Betty. What that was supposed to achieve, Dougal didn't know.

Betty's answering smile was sly. "If you don't, your rent might double, and there will be a lot of cheesed off people who can't talk me into selling to them."

"This is an outrage," Morag shouted.

Again, someone who wasn't wrong.

"I will never give you free pies," Morag declared.

Caroline cleared her throat and, as if she'd waved a magic wand, there was instant silence. *How did she do that?*

"May I suggest that we take the cost of Betty's 'free' pies from council funds? Seeing as everyone in town will benefit from this arrangement."

There was a murmur of approval, and Morag nodded before sitting back down in a huff.

"Still free for me," Betty taunted her nemesis.

Morag's two friends placed restraining hands on her as Betty blithely carried on.

"Number Three. I want a job dyeing hair at the spa."

That caused laughter. It was well known around town that

she'd been angling for that job since Jodie opened the place. It was why she'd taken to dyeing her head blue. As a sort of audition for the role.

"Not going to happen," Jodie said from where she sat next to her husband, Mitch, in the front row.

"Even if the town is goin' tae suffer because you say no?"

Jodie pinned Betty with a stare. "Not. Going. To. Happen."

The room held its collective breath as the two women stared each other down. Dougal's money was on Jodie. She was the only person he'd ever met who'd made Betty back off. If he hadn't seen it with his own eyes, he wouldn't have believed it.

"Then I want to work reception and book in all the beauty appointments," Betty said, making people gasp with the shock of seeing her cave.

"No," Jodie said.

"Then I want to wax off Dougal's beard." Betty grinned at him as he gasped, his hands automatically going to his beard as if to protect it.

Jodie stared at him, apparently considering the demand.

"Over my dead body," he said.

"That would work for me," Betty answered.

"Move on from the spa," Jodie told her. "Nothing on your list that's even vaguely related to my business is going to happen."

People in the room looked like they might pass out at the shock of Jodie's words. Getting Betty to sell would mean a lot of new opportunities for the folk in town. And watching them fall at the first hurdle was hard.

To everyone's shock, Betty just shrugged. "It was worth a try. You make a fine apprentice, lassie."

Jodie rolled her eyes. "Get on with it. Some of us have better things to do with our time than pander to your ego."

"All of us," Josh amended. "Not some. It's definitely all of us."

"Number Four," Betty said loudly, but Lake was reading over her shoulder and put out a hand to stop her.

"Don't even think about it. I will lock you up in chains before I give you a gun," he said.

She frowned at him but moved on. "Number five." Her smile put the fear of God into half the room. "I want to see Grunt's willy piercing."

When there was no outraged protest, it became clear that Grunt and his wife, Claire, were not at the meeting.

"Consider it done," Dougal lied merrily. He'd deal with the fallout later, because there was no way the mountain-sized American would let Betty near his privates.

"I'm holding you to that." She narrowed her eyes at him.

"Get on with it," he told her. "How many more items are on your list?"

"Hold yer horses," she said. "I'm getting there." She took a slow, deep breath as her eyes glinted in his direction. "Number six," she said at last. "I want the first of July to be a public holiday in my name—Betty Day."

"We can't declare a national holiday," Dougal said as he felt a headache start.

"I can live with it just being in Invertary," the evil woman said.

Dougal glanced at his fellow council members, who shrugged. It seemed nobody could see a catch in her demand, other than a day with her name on it.

"Done," Dougal said.

"And I want a parade on Betty Day."

Again, the council nodded. "Done."

"And a float filled with Chippendale dancers."

"She's determined to make a mockery of this town," Morag shouted.

Again. Not wrong.

"No Chippendales. No property sales," Betty said, then grinned. "That rhymes."

"Who are the Chippendales?" Caroline asked.

"Male strippers, baby," Josh said, making his wife blush. "You don't need to see that."

"Scared of a little competition?" Betty said. "Worried your wife will see what a dud she married?"

Before Dougal or Josh could answer, Lake put a hand on Betty's shoulder. "Enough," was all he said.

Betty rolled her eyes at him. "If you weren't the son of my heart, I'd seriously consider poisoning you. You get in the way of all my fun." She turned back to Dougal. "Am I getting my Chippendales or no'?"

He heaved a sigh. "You can have your stripper float."

Betty whooped. "Number seven," she read from her paper. "I want each of the Domino Boys to take me out for a fancy dinner in Fort William. Not together. I want a date with each of them."

"I'm married!" James shouted in protest.

"She can have you," his wife shouted back.

"Who's paying for these dinners?" Archie demanded. "I'm on a pension."

Dougal felt his heartburn start again.

"The council can pay for that too," Caroline said. "Any objections?"

"Aye," Hamish called out. "I object to having dinner with Satan."

"Overruled," Dougal boomed. "You get your dinners," he told Betty. "Now, are you done?"

"Nowhere near." She grinned.

The room groaned as one.

"Number eight. I want the women of Knit or Die to make Betty banners to be hung all over town. They need to say nice things about me. And I want those crocheted flowers on all of them."

The women slumped in their chairs but nodded at Dougal.

"Done," he said wearily.

"Number nine. I want every baby born in the next year—"

"—to be sacrificed at her Satanic alter," Josh interrupted.

Betty pointed a gnarled finger at Josh. "Wish I'd thought of that. No, I want them all to be named after me."

"Even the boys?" Mitch asked.

"Aye." Her eyes glinted with glee.

And, of course, the hall erupted with shouts of outrage. If he didn't get control of the situation fast, they'd soon have a riot on their hands. He paused, wondering who'd own the properties if Betty died in the ensuing chaos. No. He was a better man than that. It was his responsibility to keep order.

"Everybody calm down. She feeds off the anger," he shouted, and a semblance of order returned. He turned back to Betty. "You can't expect everyone to name their babies after you."

"I can, and I do. You should too if you want to build that fancy conference center of yours." She swung her short legs in glee.

"Wait." Mitch stood. "Who's due to give birth within the next year?"

"Claire," her mother, Heather, said, giving Betty the evil eye.

"It would have to be Grunt's wife," Mitch muttered. He turned to Betty. "There's no way he's going to let you name any of his kids *Betty*. And there's nobody in Invertary who can make him. You're stuffed."

"Fine." She glared at everyone. "Then I want Lake and Kirsty to change their name to McLeod."

"No!" Kirsty shot to her feet.

Lake just looked amused. He strode across the floor and whispered something in his wife's ear before returning to Betty's side. "Done," he said.

A ripple of shock ran around the room.

"You're changing your name to McLeod?" Betty said with suspicion.

"That's what you want, right?"

"Aye." She narrowed her eyes at him.

"Then done."

Everyone looked at Kirsty to see if she agreed. She just sat there, glaring at Betty.

"Well, I guess that one's taken care of, then," Dougal said. "Is that the last of it?" *Please God, let that be the last of it!*

"Nearly," Betty looked at her paper. "I want Reverend Morrison to be brought back from Spain, and I want him to stand in front of all of you and admit that we've had sex. Lots and lots of sex."

"Betty!" Caroline snapped. "There are children here."

"I know, and they all got here because their parents had sex."

"What's sex?" four-year-old Jessica asked her father, Josh.

"Uh." Josh looked at Caroline, then back at his daughter. "That's a question your mother can answer later." He lowered his voice and muttered, "Like in about twenty years."

"We can't drag the Reverend back to Scotland just so he can humiliate himself for your benefit," Dougal told the evil empress of Invertary.

"Then, I guess we're at an impasse." She dug into her bag and brought out a pie, then set about eating it, without a care in the world.

And why should she have a care? She had everyone in the room over a barrel.

"How about we get him to tell us by Skype?" Mitch suggested.

"I've seen that telly program," Betty said around a mouthful of food. "I know those videos can be faked. He needs to be here in real life. In person."

"Is this your last demand?" Dougal said. "If we get the Reverend here, will that be the end of it?"

She paused for a moment, clearly enjoying the tension. "If he tells the truth to everybody, aye."

Dougal wasn't convinced. "Then you'll negotiate the sale of your properties?"

"Aye. But you'd better bring a big fat wallet. I'll no' be letting anything go for a song."

"Mitch," Dougal snapped. "Get the contract out. I want to make sure Betty can't renege on our agreement."

"Contract?" Betty spat some food with the word.

"Aye, we drew one up that says we've met your demands, that you won't come up with any more or stall the process further, and when the last agreed upon demand is complete, you'll seriously consider any offers made on your holdings."

She looked up at Lake. "Did you know about this?"

"It was my idea," Lake said, remaining stony-faced.

"You make me so proud," Betty told him.

As Mitch led Satan over to the table in the corner, to sign their agreement, Dougal sidled up to Lake.

"Are you really going to change your name to McLeod?" he whispered.

"Absolutely." Lake nodded, a sparkle in his eye.

"What are you up to?" Dougal asked.

"She didn't say which name," Lake said. "So, we'll change our middle names. We can always change them back down the track. She isn't going to live forever."

Lake's devious mind impressed Dougal, but he was a bit worried about his reasoning. "I don't know about that," he said. "I think that witch might outlast us all."

And with that, as though Betty could hear him from

halfway across the room, she looked up, caught his eye and laughed.

A New Client for Benson Security

Callum's laptop suddenly made loud kissing noises in the middle of his meeting with Joe.

Joe grinned. "Should I worry about your relationship with that thing?"

"It's Isobel. She got into the system settings and changed the notification sound for her messages."

"The perils of working with your wife."

Callum cocked an eyebrow at Joe's perfectly pressed jeans. "You can talk."

The American just shook his head. "She thinks I should look smart for work."

"Aye, and now your jeans have a nice ironed line right down the front of them and your T-shirt smells like spring flowers." His laptop started to make X-rated gasping noises.

Joe laughed. "At least Julia only irons. You'd better answer that before your laptop has an orgasm."

With a shake of his head, Callum brought up the message screen.

Your 10.30 is here. He's seriously stuck up. Are you sure you want to see him?

"It would seem Mr. 'Brown's' here," he told Joe as he typed his reply: *Show him in. I can handle him.*

I know you can xxxxxoxxoo

He stared at her message for a second. It was a far cry from the sort of interactions he'd had back in the army. But then again, if his CO had sent him a note with kisses and hugs on it, he'd have been seriously worried. "You ready for this?" he asked.

Joe tapped the folder in front of him. "Bring it on. Let's see what this guy's playing at."

Callum turned to face the door, just as it banged open.

Isobel's face was green as she pointed to the distinguished-looking older gentleman beside her. "This is Mr. Brown." She practically pushed him through the door. "Can you take Sophie for a minute?"

Without waiting for an answer, she shoved their four-year-old into the room and ran. Dressed in a Wonder Woman costume, and with a bag of art materials under her arm, Sophie seemed completely unfazed by being dumped on them.

"Hey, gorgeous," Joe said. "Pull up a chair beside me and keep me company."

With a smile, she rounded the desk, climbed up beside Joe and started setting out her sketchpad and pens in front of her.

Meanwhile, their prospective client stood frowning after Isobel. In his late sixties, with a head of perfectly groomed white hair, he held himself with an air of confidence that only came with money and power. And with the familiarity of wielding both.

"You might want to consider hiring staff who behave in a more professional manner," he said. "Your receptionist is the first impression your company makes, and my experience thus far hasn't instilled confidence."

Callum barely contained a growl. "That *staff member* is my wife, and she's three months pregnant, which is why she ran for the toilet. It was either that or puke on the client. Which would be pretty damn unprofessional, wouldn't you agree?"

"My apologies." Mr. Brown tugged at the sleeves of his Savile Row suit before opening a button on the jacket. He looked pointedly at Joe. "I don't believe we've met."

Joe frowned and didn't bother offering his hand. "Joe Barone. I work here."

If Mr. Brown was waiting for more information, he'd be waiting a while. He might rule his little kingdom, but things ran differently in the London office of Benson Security, and he had no clout there. On top of that, he'd not only insulted Callum's pregnant wife but had made an appointment using a fake identity. Which was seriously stupid, because what sort of security company would they be if they didn't investigate their prospective clients?

"May I?" Brown pointed at a chair, his tone making it clear he felt Callum should have invited him to sit before he'd had to ask.

"Aye, take a seat." Callum was fast losing patience. Isobel was always telling him that he needed to be more polite, but this guy didn't deserve the effort. "What can we do for you?"

"Clam," Sophie snapped and handed him a drawing.

He took it and put it beside him on the pile of drawings she'd already done that morning, flashing her a smile before turning back to Mr. Brown, who was frowning at his daughter.

"I really don't think it's appropriate to discuss business in front of a child," he said.

"Don't worry. She doesn't care about anything you have to say anyway. So spit it out. What brings you to Benson Security?" He leaned forward and clasped his hands in front of him on the desk.

"I have a delicate matter to discuss regarding my company."

Joe flicked open the folder he'd compiled on their prospective client. "You mean the Ford-Talbot company TayFor Pharmaceuticals and the rumor you're losing money?"

To his credit, the fake Mr. Brown didn't blanch at being found out. "I see you've done some digging."

"Aye, we tend to do that around here, seeing as we're in the security business." Callum cocked an eyebrow at his business partner's father. "What I'd like to know is why are you here under an assumed name and why aren't you talking to your daughter, Mr. *Ford-Talbot?*"

Ford-Talbot cleared his throat. The first sign of nerves since entering Callum's office. "I thought it best to test the waters first."

"In other words, you're scared of Rachel's reaction."

He huffed out a breath, making him seem almost human. "Yes, well, you know my daughter."

Callum snorted. He did indeed. Rachel could eviscerate a man with a few well-placed words. It was actually kind of comforting to know her family wasn't exempt from her attitude.

"Clam!" Sophie thrust another drawing at him.

He glanced at it. They were getting better, but he still didn't have a clue what half of them were. That didn't stop him from keeping every single one—he even had special folders for them.

Rachel's father frowned at Sophie again before returning his attention to Callum, who just stared calmly at him. They were talking in front of Sophie or not at all. He sure as hell wasn't going to kick his daughter out of the room to please Rachel's lying father.

Ford-Talbot took a deep breath. "Mr. Barone is right. Rumors are swirling around my company. But the problem goes far deeper than the rumor we're losing money. I have come to believe my competition has infiltrated my company."

Oh, now that was more interesting than Callum had expected. He cast a glance at Joe, who was all about paying attention now that they'd gotten to the juicy part of the meeting.

"You want us to find the spies and shut their operation down," Joe said.

"Yes."

"And you don't want Rachel to know," Callum added. "I'll tell you right now, that isn't going to happen. I don't keep secrets from my business partners."

"No, that isn't my intention." Letting out a breath, Ford-Talbot pinned Callum with eyes identical to his daughter's. "I want you to talk her into taking the job. I want her to be the one investigating from inside the company."

Joe let out a low whistle. "Good luck with that."

It was well known around the office that Rachel had nothing to do with her family business, and she tore the head off anyone who asked why.

"Interesting." Callum sat back in his chair and considered the man in front of him. "At least that explains why you didn't go to one of the bigger security companies."

It was Ford-Talbot's turn to snort. "And risk the wrath of Rachel? I don't think so. My daughter mightn't want anything to do with her heritage, but she'd be furious if I took company business elsewhere."

But that didn't answer the burning question. "Why do you want Rachel to investigate? She's the last person I'd send in."

Joe nodded his agreement. "We have operatives here who are far more skilled. People who've done undercover work with intelligence agencies. They would know what to look for and have the ability to find it."

"I realize that." His eyes flicked to Sophie, and his gaze softened. "What do you know about TayFor Pharmaceuticals?"

Callum shrugged. "Boutique company. Well respected. Your R&D Department's won plenty of government grants and awards. You have a niche market and you're the best in it."

"And"—Ford-Talbot tugged at his tie in a nervous gesture that seemed out of character—"we're a family-run company."

"Ah," Joe said, glancing at Callum. "You suspect a family member might be involved."

Looking his age for the first time since he strode into the office, Ford-Talbot ran a hand down his face. "I honestly don't know, but I fear that might be the case. My son," he said and paused, "is the CEO. He's very involved in the day-to-day workings of the company. Very little gets past him."

"And that's why you need Rachel," Callum said. "No one else would be able to get close enough to the family members involved in the business."

"I'm afraid so."

There was a heavy silence, broken by Sophie getting out of her chair, stalking over to Callum, and climbing into his lap. He automatically wrapped his arms around his adopted daughter, feeling his heart melt as he did so. She placed a tiny hand on either side of his face and looked into his eyes, all somber attitude.

"Can I have ice cream? Muma said no, but you can say yes, can't you, Daddy?"

And there it was, the word that brought him to his alloy-based knees and had him wrapped around her little finger.

"We'll get some as soon as this meeting's over, okay?"

"Sucker," Joe said through a cough.

Callum scowled at Joe as Ford-Talbot smiled wistfully at him and his daughter.

The older man caught his eye. "Hard to believe that Rachel used to do that."

"Aye, very hard to believe."

Rachel's father broke eye contact and looked down at his hands. "I know you might not believe this, but I love my daughter very much. Years ago, something happened with the company that turned her away from the business and distanced her from family. I would very much like to amend that situation."

"And you think the best way to do that is to sneak in here behind her back, lying about who you are?" Joe said.

"Good point," Ford-Talbot said with a shake of his head.

The door swung open and the woman under discussion stepped into the room. As usual, she was decked out in a designer suit that must have cost the entire GDP of a small country. Her trademark black stilettos gave her an extra few inches of height and some serious attitude.

She stared down at her dad. "Father, would you like to explain why you're in my business without informing me?"

Isobel rushed in behind her, out of breath and looking gorgeous. She'd lost that gray/green sheen she had before she'd run for the bathroom. "I tried to stop her, but I was sick, and she got past me." She smacked Rachel on the arm. "Bad, Rachel! We talked about this. It's unfair to take advantage of the pregnant woman."

Rachel narrowed her eyes at Isobel, but Callum wasn't worried—his wife could take care of herself. "As soon as you push that squealing infant into the world, you and I are going to have a long *chat* about all the times you've struck me."

Isobel beamed at her. "I'm so proud of you. You used the word infant without looking disgusted." She wrapped her in a hug while Rachel stood there like a wooden board.

"Callum," Rachel said. "Do something."

"It's hormones." Callum grinned at his partner. "It should sort itself in another six months."

"Muma!" Sophie climbed off his lap. "Daddy said I can have ice cream."

"Did he now?" Releasing poor Rachel, she cast him a disparaging glance. "When are you going to stop giving her everything she wants just because she calls you Daddy?" She took Sophie's hand.

Callum couldn't answer because the truth would just embarrass him in front of their new client.

"Um," Joe said, "I think that would be round about *never*."

"Dickhead," Callum told him, receiving a grin for his effort. "Wait until you're a father. Then we'll talk."

A misty glaze filled Joe's eyes. "Speaking of which. I need to go work on that. Where's Jules?"

"She's working on the company accounts," Isobel said.

Joe grinned. "Perfect. Accounts always make her horny." He headed for the door.

"What's horny?" Sophie asked Isobel, who groaned.

"I take it this meeting's over." Ford-Talbot looked bemused.

Rachel narrowed her eyes at her father as she shut the door behind Isobel. "Oh, no. It's just beginning." She looked at Callum. "And I'll deal with you later."

He held up his hands. "I was going to tell you. He's the one who came here under an assumed name. I'm innocent in this."

"Of course you are." She sat down and crossed her legs before glaring at her father. "Start at the beginning. Why exactly do you need Benson Security's help?"

"Oh, it's much worse than that, darling," her father said. "I need your help."

Valentine's Day at Glasgow School of Art

It was Donna's first Valentine's Day as a married woman, and she'd hoped for a romantic evening with Duncan. Unfortunately, a Glasgow School of Art faculty meeting meant he was busy, and she was stuck entertaining her sister Mairi, who was visiting from Campbeltown. It was not how she'd planned to spend the evening. And it was going downhill rapidly.

"I'm going to get into so much trouble," Donna said as she led Mairi down the worn stone steps into the basement of the Mackintosh building. "I can't believe you talked me into this."

"You can't?" Mairi said. "Really? *You* can't believe you were talked into this? Say that again so I can film it for Aggie and Isobel." She held up her phone.

Donna stopped on the stairs below her sister. "Do you want to go to the life drawing class or not?"

She hurriedly tucked the phone back into her jeans pocket. "Do I want to sit in a room with a hot naked man and pretend to draw him? Yes. I definitely want to do that."

Donna groaned. She should never have shown her sister

the drawings from her last class. The model had been a post-grad student who played rugby in his spare time. To Donna, he'd been a chance to study defined muscle form. To her sister, he was a chance to perv over a hot, naked guy. There was no way this evening was going to end well.

"This is so wrong. Life drawing isn't about perving over the model. It's about drawing the human form. Artists don't even see the model as a person. They might as well be drawing a bowl of fruit."

"You mean like a banana and two plums?"

"You're sick in the head. You do know that, right?"

"And proud of it."

They turned the corner out of the stairwell and headed for the basement studio that housed the early evening life class. The newly painted white walls on either side of them were art free, but that would soon change as students pinned up their work. Then, in another six months or so, they would need a new whitewash and the cycle would start all over again.

"What does Keir think you're doing right now?" Donna said. "Because you definitely didn't tell him you were pretending to be an artist just to ogle the model."

"I told him the truth," Mairi said. "That I was going to Glasgow to spend some quality time with my sister in order to find out more about her new life as an artist."

"And he believed you?"

"Keir and I have an understanding. I tell him what I want him to believe, and he has to figure out what the reality is. It's like a game. It keeps things interesting."

Mairi's relationship was a mystery to her sisters.

"Didn't he wonder why you weren't spending Valentine's Day with him?" Donna wished she was spending it with Duncan.

"No. He knows what I think about it."

She was almost afraid to ask. "Which is?"

"It's all about sex. You eat chocolate, drink champagne, and talk romantic crap to each other—all in the hopes of getting laid. Keir knows I'm a sure thing, and that makes Valentine's Day a waste of effort."

"That has to be the most romantic thing I've ever heard," Donna said sarcastically.

"I should write for Hallmark," Mairi agreed.

They pushed through the heavy wooden door—scarred and splattered with paint from years of use—and into the plain white windowless room. There were already several people inside. Some stood chatting while others dragged their stools into position or set up easels. They called out their hellos to her and Donna smiled back. There was no way to feel like an outsider in this group. There were eighteen-year-olds straight from school, and people in their sixties studying in retirement. There was every background, class and color. And they all had one thing in common—a passion for art.

"Where do we sit?" Mairi stage whispered. "Will the model pose on that stool in the middle? Which way will he be facing? I want to be in front."

Donna felt her face heat as she caught a fellow student's eye.

"She's keen," he said with a twinkle in his eye. Bernard was a retired postman and a wonderful painter. He'd also seen right through Mairi. So much for her pretending to be an artist.

"She's my sister." Donna leaned toward him. "She made me bring her. I don't think she can even draw a straight line."

His smile was pure mischief. "Don't worry. I don't think she's here for the art."

"No kidding..." She turned to find Mairi carrying a stool

around the room as she asked everyone which the best place was to set up for a 'good full frontal.'

"Kill me now," Donna muttered, making Bernard laugh.

From behind a partition at the back of the room, their model stepped out. Donna let out a groan—it was the same athletic guy from the week before. Ever since Mairi had invited herself along, she'd been silently praying for another model. *Any* other model.

"If I left now," she said to Bernard. "Would you mind keeping an eye on my sister for me?"

"Not on your life!" He grinned.

"Wow," Mairi said to the woman beside her. "This art school doesn't skimp on the models." She cleared her throat and smiled at Gareth, their model. "Do you know which way you'll be facing? I want to get a good spot."

The post-grad student didn't smile back. "This is a life class. Every spot is a good one. It's all about the drawing. If you want to learn, choose a difficult angle, and start with some loose sketches, focusing on general form and light. What medium are you using? Charcoal? Pastel?"

Mairi looked flummoxed as she held up a pencil.

Gareth shook his head. "Charcoal is better for fast sketching. Easier to smudge out the mistakes. Anybody got any charcoal they can give the new girl?"

Mairi stepped toward him. "Between you and me, I'm *so* new that it's probably a good idea for me to just observe this week—from the front. I mean, your front. So you can give me tips while I stare at you. I mean study you. In an artistic way."

She was going to get them both killed. As soon as Keir figured out what she was up to, they were dead.

Donna hurried across the room, grabbed her sister's arm, and smiled apologetically at Gareth. "Don't mind her. She hit her head on the way here."

She dragged her sister to the back of the room. "Will you behave? You're going to get me kicked out. Or worse, a reputation as a pervert. You said you'd quietly observe. Nothing else."

"You know"—Mairi put her hands on her hips—"I don't think I like this new, assertive Donna."

"If you don't behave, I'll assert my right to drag you out of here by the hair."

"I'm telling Aggie you said that."

"Good evening," a voice called out, and the class turned to find their tutor standing in the doorway.

And she wasn't alone.

Behind her, arms folded and glares in place, were their men.

"Oh, crap, we're busted," Mairi said. "And there aren't even any windows in here to make an escape."

Donna wasn't listening, she was too busy crumbling under Duncan's stare. She pointed at her sister. "She made me do it!"

"I know," Duncan said.

"We all know," Keir said.

"Even me," Bernard, the fink, added.

"How did you get here so fast from Campbeltown?" Mairi asked, because *that* was the most important issue at hand. Not the fact Donna had most likely broken a million school rules sneaking her into class. Or that she'd probably made the model feel objectified by doing so.

She shot Gareth an apologetic smile, and he shook his head at her—disappointed. Her stomach clenched. She could cope with anything better than she could cope with disappointment.

"Rusty," Keir said with a shake of his head. "I followed you up here after I heard you bullying Donna into bringing you."

"You listened to my private calls?" Her indignation caused

a burst of laughter from the other students. Keir just rolled his eyes.

"Gareth," their tutor said. "You're being swapped out this evening. Don't worry, you won't lose your money." She turned to Duncan. "Do you want to do the honors?"

He swung the door open and a tiny, wrinkled old man sauntered in. "Meet your new model," Duncan said.

A cheer went up at the sight of the popular model. There was nothing like the challenge of drawing someone who wasn't perfect, someone with Stuart's lines and wrinkles.

Unfortunately for her, Mairi wasn't an artist. "Okay," she said. "I'm done here."

"Not so fast, Picasso," Duncan said. "The art faculty want to encourage your new-found interest in life drawing, and we *insist* that you stay for the whole class. Isn't that right, Rhonda?" He inclined his head toward the tutor.

"I can't wait to see your drawings." She gave Mairi a wide smile.

Mairi headed for the door. "I wouldn't want to impose, and I should really spend time with my fiancé. It is Valentine's Day, and he's come all this way to see me."

"Don't worry," Keir said as he blocked her escape. "We will be spending time together. Duncan gave me permission to attend class with you and make sure you got the full art-school experience." He glanced at the old guy. "Which way are you facing? We want to make sure we're right in front and close enough to see every hair on your chest."

The old man cackled. "That's up to the teacher, but I'm sure she won't mind you taking the front row."

"Not at all," Rhonda said, clearly enjoying herself.

"Keir." Mairi batted her eyelashes at her husband. "There's been a misunderstanding. I was only here to support Donna."

"Sure you were."

"Donna," she called, "tell him!"

"She can't." Duncan wrapped an arm around Donna and swept her through the door. "My wife has other plans for the evening."

"I wasn't flirting," Mairi shouted.

"I know," Keir said. "You don't flirt. You were ogling. So, now you can ogle Stuart. He's cool with it, aren't you, Stuart?"

The old guy winked at Mairi.

The door shut behind them, blocking Mairi's outrage and everyone else's laughter. It was suddenly very quiet in the corridor. And much smaller than it had been when she'd walked along it to get to class. Donna wondered if that was because Duncan's shoulders were unnaturally wide, or if he just grew in size when he was mad.

He cocked an eyebrow at her. "What did we agree?"

She shuffled uncomfortably as she shifted her sketchpad under her arm. "That if I felt I couldn't say no to someone, if I felt cornered, I'd ask you for help." She looked up at him. "But that wasn't meant for my sisters."

"Angel," he said on a sigh. "It was definitely meant for your sisters."

"Oh." She studied her feet. "Did I break an art school rule taking her to class?" She pressed a hand to her stomach, sick at the thought.

"No, but we like to keep the classes for art students, not for folk after a cheap thrill."

Her stomach tightened further. "Do you think the other students are going to be mad at me?" An even worse thought occurred to her, and she felt the blood drain from her face. "Will I be reprimanded for turning Gareth into a sexual object for my sister? Is that assault? Will I be arrested?"

Duncan raised his head and looked over her shoulder. "Gareth?" he called.

Donna almost sank into the floor when she realized the

model was behind her. She hadn't even heard the studio door open.

"Do you feel like a sexual object?" he asked the student.

"Not nearly often enough," Gareth said with a grin, before sauntering off.

"Gareth seems fine," Duncan said drolly.

"Did I get you into trouble?" That was the last thing she wanted to do.

"Come here." Duncan pulled her into his arms, and she felt her stomach settle. "You didn't get me into trouble." His voice rumbled through her.

"I'm sorry," Donna said. "I'll talk to Mairi and make sure this doesn't happen again."

"Oh, don't worry about your sister." He sounded amused. "Keir's taking care of her. After an hour drawing Stuart, she'll be begging you to keep her away from here. I asked him to make sure she got the best view possible, for each and every pose."

"Was Keir upset?"

He barked out a laugh. "This is the least of the things he has to deal with when it comes to your sister." He turned them toward the lift. "Come on, you can keep me company while I finish up in my studio."

It was a subdued Donna that followed him up to the top floor. Through the glass walls that made up the hen run—a passageway that ran over the gallery roofs to the east side of the building—Donna watched the lights of the city flicker in the darkness. It always took her breath away to see so many of them dancing in the night. For a small-town girl, seeing the vastness of the city sometimes made her feel as though she'd been swallowed whole.

Duncan led her to his studio, unlocked the door and pushed it wide. As she stepped inside, the glow of countless candles—almost as many as the lights of the city—met her.

She stopped dead at the sight of a picnic blanket in the middle of the paint-splattered wooden floor. There was chocolate cake, strawberries, and champagne. But no roses. Those would always remind them both of his first wife, Fiona. Instead, there was a vase of tall sunflowers, their faces so rich in gold and orange that her fingers itched to touch.

Strong arms wound around her waist, and his chin rested on her shoulder. "I'm sorry I had to attend the staff meeting tonight. I'd planned on bringing you up here *after* your class. It isn't anything special, but I wanted you to know that I'd thought of you." He pressed a kiss to the sensitive crook of her neck. "You're always on my mind, Angel."

Tears welled in Donna's eyes as she clung to her husband. She would never get used to having him all to herself. Some days, it felt like she'd been blessed beyond her capacity to handle it.

"It's perfect," she said.

He turned her in his arms and cradled her to him. "I thought that after we'd eaten and I'd plied you with champagne, that I could talk you into posing naked for me. I want to see you here, right in the center of my studio, and to immortalize that sight in paint. And then I want to remember it every time I come into this room."

All she could do was whisper his name.

As his lips descended to hers, Donna thought that Valentine's Day had turned out so much better than she'd expected it to. And the night had only just begun

Jack's Next Step

"Is she still crying?" Jack asked when he heard the window open behind him.

It was late at night, and he was sitting in his usual spot—on the roof outside his bedroom window. Since moving to London from the middle-of-nowhere, Scotland, Jack could often be found looking out over the city while he listened to the constant hum of all those people. Going from a town of about a hundred folk to a city the size of London had been a shock to his system. But not an unwelcome one. Life in London was a million times better.

"No, she stopped crying a wee while ago." His stepdad, Callum, climbed out onto the roof beside him. "Now, she's playing with her Barbies." He cast a sideways glance at Jack, his eyes sparkling. "They're torturing G.I. Joe for leaving them to go into the army."

He couldn't help but laugh. His five-year-old sister, Sophie, was resilient. She might not like that he was going away for army training, but she'd find a way to cope.

"You all packed?" Callum stretched out his legs in front of him and rested back on his elbows.

"Yep." He grinned at the only man who'd ever been a father to him, even if had only been for the past few, far too short, years. "And then Mum repacked my bag."

Callum shook his head, a smile on his face. "Did you redo it?"

"Had to. She doesn't have a clue how to pack."

"Tell me about it."

They sat in silence, looking out over the rooftops of Chelsea. To one side of them, at the end of the garden, stood the old terraced building that housed the London office of Benson Security—the business Callum owned with his partners.

"Few years and I'll be working in there with you." Jack lifted his chin toward the building.

"I'm counting on it."

The confident reply settled something within him. "Mum's still hoping I'll change my mind."

Callum smiled as he stared out into the night. "She wouldn't be Isobel if she didn't. To her, you're still the wee boy she had to care for all on her own, even though she was barely a girl herself. For eighteen years, her life's been all about keeping you out of danger. It's hard for her to see you walk into a situation that's the opposite."

"But the army will train me for anything that comes my way. And I already know how to look after myself." Probably more so than any of the other recruits in his class. Because Jack had spent two years training with Callum and the other ex-military personnel at Benson Security. He had a black belt in Karate and was on his way to one in Krav Maga. On top of that, he knew his way around a series of firearms, had basic knowledge of how to function in a tactical situation, and was pretty decent in a knife fight. He was prepared, at peak fitness, and had support and experience at his back, giving him a quiet confidence most kids his age didn't possess. That he was even aware of the difference between himself and his fellow recruits spoke volumes.

In other words, he was lucky, and he knew it.

"Being trained doesn't stop crap from happening." Callum pointed at his legs.

If anyone knew that to be true, it was Callum. Under his jeans were two state-of-the-art prosthetic limbs. He'd lost his legs after bombing while on an operation with the SAS.

"I could also step off the curb tomorrow and get hit by a bus," Jack said.

"Especially in London," Callum said with a grin.

They lapsed into another comfortable silence, each lost in their thoughts. In the distance, a siren wailed as the constant noise of London ebbed and flowed around them.

"Do you think I'll make it?" he couldn't help but ask. "Or do you think I'll wash out of training?"

"I don't *think* you'll make it," Callum said. "I *know* you will. And I also know that you'll be one of the finest paratroopers the unit's ever seen."

Jack blinked hard as his eyes began to sting; he blamed it on the London air—the only downside of living in the capital. "Not sure I'll live up to your reputation though," he joked.

Callum McKay was a legend within the parachute regiment. One that had gone on to join the exclusive ranks of the SAS. It was a path Jack hoped to follow, but he was more than aware he had big shoes to fill.

"Son." Callum's serious tone made Jack look him in the eye. And the intensity he saw there made his breath hitch. "You are going to surpass me in every way. And I couldn't be prouder."

Jack cleared his throat and looked away. "Got to make it through thirty-nine weeks of training first."

"There is that," Callum let him lighten the mood. "Have you said goodbye to your girl?"

Jack nodded. "Yesterday."

"The army's hard on relationships. Having a man who's always away can make a woman wonder if she'd be better off on her own, or with a guy who isn't in the military."

"Is that what happened to your first marriage?"

"Aye. That and we got into things a bit too young."

Jack knew all about taking on responsibility far too young —he was the child of a teenage mother. And, as much as he loved his mum and thought she'd done an amazing job bringing him up, he wanted to experience life before he had to deal with being responsible for someone else, whether a wife or a kid.

"I know this sounds nasty," he confessed, "but I don't think Shelley and I are gonna survive my training. And, I'm okay with that. I mean, I like her, but she isn't..."

"The one?" Callum cocked an eyebrow at him.

"Aye." Jack's shoulders slumped. "If there is such a thing as *the one*."

"Oh, there is. It just takes some doing to find them, not to mention a whole lot of luck that you'll recognize them when you see them."

"Mum?" He held his breath as he waited for the answer.

"Aye. Your mother's it for me. I'd do anything for that woman." Callum looked at Jack. "And for you kids. I might not have given you my genetics, but as far as I'm concerned, you're one hundred percent mine. You and little Sophie. You're both mine."

It was hard to speak through a tightening throat. "And the baby."

"Aye." He smiled widely. "And the baby."

"I'm glad Sophie has a sister close to her age. I would have liked a brother when I was a kid."

"So would I," Callum said. He shifted and reached into his

jeans pocket. "I've got something for you." He took out a small round brass tin and handed it to Jack.

The tin was a bit battered and scratched but had obviously been cleaned and polished. There was an engraved pattern on the top and a maker's stamp on the bottom. Jack flicked the clasp, and it popped open to reveal an old compass.

"It was my dad's," Callum said. "I took it with me on all my missions. It brought me luck."

Jack couldn't help but grin. "Callum, you lost your legs on a mission."

"Aye, but losing my legs led me to your mother. And to you and your sister. That's bloody good luck; there's no denying it." He cleared his throat. "My advice? Keep it in the pocket over your heart. Maybe it will stop a bullet."

"Kind of hoping the flak jacket will do that."

"Son, a flak jacket isn't a bulletproof vest, I thought I'd taught you that."

Jack grinned to let Callum know he was messing with him.

"Anyway," Callum said with a matching grin. "You can't engrave a flak jacket."

Jack's eyes snapped back to the compass, and there on the inside of the lid were three names: Donal, Callum, Jack. Beside each name was a date, and Jack immediately recognized the one next to his—the day he'd start his army training.

"No last names," Callum said. "That can get you into trouble in some places."

He nodded. "No. Last names would be bad." His hand wrapped tight around the cold metal case. "Thanks," he whispered.

Callum just nodded, and they stared back out across the city for a minute.

"I got you something too," Jack said. "Gimme a minute to get it."

He scrambled across the roof, ducked behind Callum, and back through the window into his room. As usual, everything was neatly in place. He wasn't sure if his urge to keep things orderly was from years of having very little or from being around military types so much. Either way, it was easy to find what he wanted. A minute later, he climbed back out onto the tiled roof and sat beside Callum.

"Here." He thrust the gift at him.

Callum took it with a look of confusion. "This is your passport. You're going to need that, son."

"Just look inside." Nerves made Jack's stomach clench, and his palms became clammy enough for him to rub them on his jeans. Although he didn't want to watch Callum open the passport, he couldn't tear his eyes from him either.

And because he was staring right at the man, he didn't miss the jolt that passed through Callum's body when he flicked to the page with Jack's details on it.

"Bloody hell," he said, sounding strangled. "When?"

Jack ran a hand down his face and swallowed hard. "Couple of months ago. By deed poll. I was just waiting for my passport to turn up to show you."

"Bloody hell," Callum repeated, still staring down at the passport as it shook in his hand.

"Is it..." Jack cleared his throat. "Is it okay? You're not mad, or anything?"

"What?" Callum's chin lifted, and his eyes met Jack's. "Best bloody gift ever." He shook his head as his eyes pooled. "Best. Right up there with your mother saying *I do*. And news of the baby. Best bloody gift."

"Good. Good." Jack nodded and blinked several times. "I wasn't sure...you know...I guess, I thought, maybe I should have asked first."

"No." Callum's arm shot out, and he clasped the nape of Jack's neck. "You didn't need to ask. I don't just call you son because I'm decades older. I call you son because that's what you are to me. That's what you'll always be. Even if your mother and I, God forbid, ever split up, you will still be *my* son. So this"—he waved the passport—"this is bloody perfect." He looked back down at the passport, sniffed and grinned. "Jack McKay sounds good, eh?"

"Yeah," Jack agreed.

Callum's hand flexed on Jack's neck as he looked back up at him. "Thank you for this gift. I love you, son." He tugged Jack forward and wrapped and arm around him, pounding his back in a firm hug.

"I love you too," Jack whispered, "...Dad."

Dear Abby

Dear Abby,

You are the love of my life.

"You're really going to write her a letter about this?" Flynn's thirteen-year-old daughter shook her head as she looked over his shoulder.

Flynn Boyle held up the card he'd spent good money on. "It isn't a letter. It's a huge, sparkly card. With. Hearts."

She gave him a pitying look. "It won't work. And you can't start it like that. It's really corny."

Flynn let out a frustrated growl and tried again.

Dear Abby,

~~*You are the love of my life.*~~ *You're the most amazing woman I know.*

"Still corny," Katy said.

"If you aren't going to help, you need to get lost."

She put a hand on his back, tossed her plaited hair over her shoulder, and gave him the kind of superior look only a newly minted teenager could deliver. "A hand-written note won't get you out of this mess. Maybe you should take her

"

away somewhere, like Paris. Or the moon. Somewhere she can't see what you've done."

"Helpful. Really helpful." He eyed her Invertary Juniors soccer strip. "Why aren't you at practice?"

"Because the coach is here, screwing up his marriage."

"Your mother will kill me if she hears you saying screwing."

"Then you need to stop saying it too. You're setting a bad example."

"And that's still no excuse for missing practice. Serious football players put in the work. You know that."

"What's the point? There's hardly any opportunity for me to play anyway. Apart from our tiny league, there's nothing for girls around here. There's no girls' team at school, and they won't let me join the boys' team—even though I am way better than all their other players put together."

Damn right she was. "Don't worry. I'm dealing with that. By the time my lawyers are finished with your school, they'll be begging you to captain their boys' team. Which is why you can't miss any practices, and why I asked Harry to cover for me while I deal with this."

"Uncle Harry doesn't know squat about football. We both know that he'll have the team stay inside and play FIFA International Soccer online, while he calls it a strategy session."

She had a point.

"Go away. I need to concentrate. Go find your sisters and annoy them."

"Um, they're busy playing with your new acquisition." She pointed at the wall of windows overlooking the garden, to the paddock beyond, where the two seven-years-olds were adding bows to the latest animal he'd been conned into rescuing.

"How does this keep happening to me?" Flynn groaned.

Katy patted his back. "It's because you're a soft touch.

You shouldn't have done that interview with *Cosmo* where you told the world all about the animals you rescue. I told you it was a bad idea. Now everybody wants you to take on their unwanted pets because you're rich enough to look after them and you're easy to con. At least before that interview, the begging phone calls only came from locals. Now we're getting them from all over Europe. I picked up the phone the other day and someone asked me about a monkey—in French!"

"I did the interview to spread the word about responsible animal ownership." He'd wanted to use his fame from his footballing days to promote a worthy cause. One that was dear to his heart, now he was a newly minted veterinarian. What the hell was wrong with that?

"It was *Cosmo*, Dad. They didn't care about your *cause*, all they cared about was getting you shirtless and comparing you to Beckham. Which, by the way, was disgusting. You need to keep your clothes on."

"Bloody Beckham. I hate that smug bastard. And there's no competition; I look way better than he does, and that's without all the makeup and tattoos he needs to look pretty. Plus, I was a better player than he ever managed to be, even on his good days. Which weren't many. Do I have to remind you about that red card? In a World Cup game? A game he could have helped his team win if he hadn't been such a dickhead and got kicked off the field. Okay, so he was playing for England, and national pride forbids any decent Scot from supporting their World Cup efforts, but as a professional footballer, I was affronted. He played like a wean throwing a tantrum. That kind of thing makes us all look bad. And don't even get me started on that 'magic left foot' of his. Magic, my arse." He glanced out the window and shot to his feet. "Crap!" He raced for the doors, threw them open and shouted, "Fergus Boyle, stop painting the alpacas!"

His four-year-old grinned at him but carried right on where he'd left off.

Flynn hung his head. "This is my life."

"I blame Claire and Megan," Katy said with the wisdom of a seen-it-all, done-it-all, thirteen-year-old. "You shouldn't have let them tell the story about the time they dyed Mrs. Baxter's sheep pink."

"I blame lack of birth control," Flynn muttered. Then he lifted his T-shirt to check his abs. Aye, still better than Beckham's.

"I'm back," Abby shouted from the front of the house.

Flynn spun to face his daughter. "I'll give you twenty pounds if you keep the kids out of the way until I break the news to your mother."

Her eyes narrowed. "Fifty, and I'll take away Fergus' paints."

"Done." Bloody terrorist.

She held out her hand. "Cash up front."

He narrowed his eyes at her as he dug his wallet out of his back pocket. "No trust. I would have been good for it. As you keep reminding me, I'm still sitting on a pile of gold from my footballing days." And from the odd advertising campaign— just to keep up awareness of his causes. It had absolutely *nothing* to do with reminding the world he was still there and looking damn good too.

He slapped a fifty into her palm. "Run. I'll head her off." And then he jogged out of the dining room and through the house to intercept his wife.

His breath caught in his throat as it usually did whenever he saw her after she'd been out of his sight for any length of time. Hell, all it took was five minutes apart, he was that gone on his wife. Had there ever been a more beautiful woman? With her long chestnut hair and her peaches-and-cream complexion, she was a sexier version of

Kate Middleton, and way better looking than Beckham's Posh.

"Hey, gorgeous." Flynn wrapped an arm around her waist and tugged her to him. "How was your day?"

He looked down into her wide eyes and stilled. She looked shocked, or worried, maybe afraid. Whatever it was, it wasn't good. His hold on her tightened. "What's wrong?"

Abby licked her lips and blinked up at him. "Don't be mad."

And just like that, his blood pressure shot right up. "Did you crash the car? Are you hurt?" He looked through the glass in the front door behind her, but the car seemed fine.

"No." She glanced away, her usually pink cheeks paling. "Maybe we should sit down? How about a nice cup of tea?"

He looked at her, his eyes narrowing as his heart raced. Something was very wrong. The last time she'd looked like this was when…

His knees gave way and he plopped back onto the stairs behind him. "No," he groaned as he ran a hand through his hair.

She sat close beside him on the stairs, her hand on his leg, patting him. "This is all your fault," she said gently, making his eyes jerk up to look at her.

"What?"

She smiled at him. That angel smile of hers that she only pulled out when she wanted to get away with murder. "I told you to use a condom, but you said, 'it'll be fine.' You were wrong."

"We can't have more children," he whined. "We can barely cope with the four we have."

"I know." She wrapped an arm around his waist and rested her head on his shoulder. "It will be okay. We'll manage."

He sighed and pulled her into his lap, wrapping his arms around her. "How far along are you?"

"Fourteen weeks."

He shook his head. "I thought you were just getting fat."

"Flynn!" She smacked his shoulder.

"What?"

"Women don't like it when you call them fat."

"I didn't call you fat. Plus, any man worth his salt likes a little junk in the trunk."

She shook her head at him before snuggling in closer. "You're the reason the kids are wild, you know that, don't you?"

He wasn't even going to deign to answer that. Instead, he stroked her silken hair and tried to get his head around the fact he was going to be a father—for the fifth time. On the plus side, Beckham only had four kids. Just one more way he trumped the bastard—virility. The thought perked him up no end, and he couldn't wait to Instagram the latest proof of his masculinity.

"You're thinking about David Beckham again, aren't you?" Abby said.

"What? No." Maybe he'd call him later, just to catch up...

"You're not mad about the pregnancy, are you? It wasn't on purpose. We agreed no more kids, and I meant it. This was just the antibiotics messing with the pill."

"No, I'm not mad. Just shocked." And thinking he probably should have worn a condom.

She wriggled in his lap, looking up at him. "Love you," she said. And there it was, the look in her eye she only got when she looked at him. The one that had him wrapped around her little finger and doing every single thing she ever wanted.

"Love you too." Loving Abby was like breathing. He needed it to live.

Damn, he should have put that in the card.

With a knowing smile, she leaned in and pressed her lips to his. And, just like that, they went up in flames. The kiss became hungry, desperate, and all other thoughts fled from Flynn's mind. Abby broke the kiss and pressed her forehead to his, letting out a needy little sigh that had him fighting the urge to carry her upstairs and finish what they'd started.

"This is exactly how we got into this situation to begin with," she said.

And at that moment, Flynn honestly didn't care. He nuzzled her throat. "Katy's watching the monsters. Let's go upstairs and celebrate." He hoped to get her into a state of total satiation before he told her his news. That way, she would be too worn out to protest.

"I can't believe I'm pregnant again," she said.

A grin broke out as the excitement of the situation hit him. "We can cope with another kid. It's all good." He felt her body tense, and his stomach clenched. "Abby?"

Big brown eyes looked up at him. "Um, I had a scan. And..." She smiled at him. "Congratulations! It's twins!"

"Twins!" He shot to his feet, toppling her out of his lap, but making sure he steadied her before glaring down at her. "Twins?"

"It's not *my* fault. They run in *your* family."

"Twins?!"

"Take a deep breath. Everything will be fine."

"Six kids? Are we trying to birth our own football team here?" He pinched the bridge of his nose and forced himself to breathe evenly. Nope. It didn't work. He still felt like his head was about to explode. "Six kids?!"

"Calm down." Abby folded her arms. "You're always saying we have plenty of room to expand."

"With animals! I was talking about animals."

"Well, now we're expanding our family too. You just need to act like an adult and deal with it."

He glared at her. "I adopted an elephant, and I'm not sorry."

"An elephant?"

"A small one. It's Indian. Ex-circus."

"An elephant?!"

"You just need to act like an adult and deal with it."

"An elephant!"

There may have been steam coming out of her ears, and he had a passing thought that her reaction might not be good for the babies. Then he reminded himself that the word was *babies* and not *baby*, and he lost his mind all over again. "I planned to tell you in a sparkly card, but you got pregnant and ruined it."

"You can't adopt an elephant."

"If you can have twins, I can have an elephant." And he needed to check on it to make sure the girls hadn't turned it into a princess with pink freaking bows.

"Will you listen to yourself?" Abby strode behind him, the heels of her peekaboo nude pumps tapping on the wooden floor. "The twins are yours too. It takes two to make babies. And you should have worn a damn condom when I told you to."

Flynn slammed through the back door and out into the garden, where Katy had let the twins and the elephant into the yard. It had pink ribbons tied around its trunk, and a Disney blanket with Dumbo on it draped over its back. It was embarrassing—for Flynn and the elephant.

"I keep telling them the elephant's a boy, but they don't care," Katy said.

"It's a real elephant," Abby said behind him.

Flynn rolled his eyes. What had she been expecting? No. Don't think the word expecting. Don't think about twins. Don't think about yet more kids painting his animals.

"Fergus! What the hell?"

"Don't curse at the children," Abby snapped. "Oh." She covered her mouth with her hand and giggled.

Because, painted on the side of the elephant, in wobbly letters, was the word *Elifart*.

"You were supposed to take his paints," Flynn said to Katy.

"He threatened to paint me, and I decided you weren't paying me enough money to deal with that."

Two ostriches ran past the fence, both wearing sparkly blue bows. Behind Flynn, a three-legged turtle made its way to the rabbit compound, where giant bunnies munched their way through a ton of lettuce. A donkey brayed in the distance before chasing two miniature horses. And the goat was eating the laundry from the line.

He felt Abby's arm snake around his waist, and he tugged her under his shoulder. If they could cope with this, they could cope with anything. "We can do two more," he told her.

"Never doubted it," she said.

"Two more what?" The twins said at the same time.

And Flynn and Abby burst out laughing, which became a little hysterical when a sheep strolled past with a chicken on its back.

A Glossary of Characters

Lake Benson: Retired English SAS soldier. He has blond hair, blue eyes, and a lip twitch that passes for a smile. He's known for his shoulder muscles and his taciturn nature. He grew up in a commune with hippy-dippy parents and rebelled by joining the establishment. He's closest to his youngest sister, Rainne, and he's married to Kirsty. He is the owner and founder of Benson Security—a reputable international security firm.

Kirsty Benson (nee Campbell): Now married to Lake Benson. She's an ex-lingerie model who runs her own lingerie shop and designs lingerie. She has scars down half her body from a car wreck. Her mum is Margaret Campbell, and her best friend is Caroline McInnes.

Josh McInnes: American singer who croons like Sinatra. He's married to Caroline, and they have a baby girl. He owns Invertary Castle, where he's now based. His best friend and manager is Mitch Harris.

Caroline McInnes (nee Patterson): Was the town's librarian until she met Josh. Now, as well as being a full-time mum, she's on the town's *un*official council, the restoration society, and the Christmas market committee.

Jena Donaldson (nee Morgan): Ex-go-go dancer from Atlantic City. She's accident prone, which hasn't stopped her taking up a new career as a DIY expert in Invertary. She's married to Matt Donaldson.

Matt Donaldson: Invertary's only cop. He has twin younger sisters—Claire and Megan—and he's cousin to Flynn and Harry Boyle.

Claire Dayton (nee Donaldson): Matt's younger sister who, along with her twin, Megan, has caused chaos in Invertary for years. She's a kindergarten teacher, has a fondness for dyeing sheep luminous pink, and is married to Grunt.

Grunt (Samuel Dayton): Grunt got his nickname thanks to his taciturn ways. He's a huge ex-marine who terrifies the living daylights out of everyone but melts when he's around his wife, Claire. He came to Scotland from America on a security job and stayed when he fell for Claire. His best friend, Joe Barone, came with him.

Flynn Boyle: Cousin to Megan, Claire, and Matt. Older brother of Harry. Flynn was a professional football player until an injury ruined his career and sent him home to Invertary. He's married to Abby, has a stepdaughter, Katy, and twin girls on the way. He's also a soft touch for unwanted animals and is studying to be a vet.

Abby Boyle (nee McKenzie): The widowed mother of Katy. Abby moved from England with her husband only to be left raising their baby and running a business on her own when he died of a brain tumor. She's now married to Flynn and pregnant with twins.

Katy McKenzie: She's five in Bad Boy, and she rules her world.

Harry Boyle: The geeky computer-genius younger brother of Flynn. He's cousin to Matt, Megan, and Claire.

Harry went to university far too young and made only one friend but started a very successful security software company. He returned home to Invertary to win the heart of his childhood crush, Magenta, whom he's now married. Harry joined forces with security expert Lake Benson to start a new international security company.

Magenta Boyle (nee Fraser) (Maggie to those who hate her): Magenta is the town's only goth. She's bad-tempered, sarcastic, and fiercely loyal. She works part time in Kirsty's lingerie shop, and the rest of the time she runs her own business as a caving guide. She's an expert on the local mines.

Rainne Benson (Rainbow): Lake's younger sister, named by the same hippie parents. She grew up in a commune and didn't have any formal schooling as a child. She's recently earned a business studies qualification and now works for an insurance firm in Glasgow. She's engaged to Alastair.

Alastair Stewart: Alastair co-owns Invertary's hunting and fishing shop with his dad. He's an expert salmon fisherman who's won lots of awards. He's currently living in Glasgow with Rainne, his fiancée.

Megan Raast (nee Donaldson): Twin sister to Claire, younger sister to Matt, cousin of Harry and Flynn. Married to Dimitri. Megan's been trying to find her way in life for years. She's worked as a salesperson, a hairdressing apprentice, a kitchen hand, a pastry chef...you name it. She's now decided her calling is security work and has moved to London to work for the new Benson Security office.

Dimitri Raast: Up until recently, he was a US Army Ranger. He quit to hunt for his missing, presumed kidnapped, sister. He joined forces with Benson Security to bring down the man who took his sister and get her back. He's married to Megan, and they're partners at work too.

Reverend Morrison: The Presbyterian vicar is about four hundred years old and doesn't give a damn what anyone thinks of him. He's one of Betty McLeod's nemeses—although Betty has hinted on more than one occasion that they're having a secret affair. He has now retired to Spain.

Betty McLeod: Betty's in her eighties. She's never been married and is alienated from her sister who lives in Glasgow. She is known locally as Satan for her evil interference in the lives of Invertary's townsfolk. She used to run the town's only underwear shop—until Kirsty opened hers and ruined it. She sold the building to Lake with the proviso that she gets the run of the place. She's now the mascot for a security firm and is learning interrogation techniques in her free time.

The Domino Boys: A group of men in their 70s and 80s who get together to gossip and play dominoes. Archie, Hamish, James and Findlay helped Caroline organize her wedding. They often fight with Betty.

Knit or Die: A knitting group that gets involved in other activities around town—like breaking into underwear shops and torturing men! They comprise of Kirsty's mother, Margaret Campbell; Matt's mother, Heather Donaldson; as well as Jean, Shona, Agnes, and Moira.

Dougal Jamieson: Dougal owns the town's only pub/hotel. He looks like Father Christmas, dresses like Elton John, and is the unofficial town mayor (unofficial because no one turned out to vote for the town council, but they do the job anyway). He has a booming voice and penchant for gossip. He also has a kind heart.

Mitch Harris: Mitch is Josh's best friend. They grew up together in Atlantic City. He's now a trained lawyer who works full time as Josh's manager. He's a ruthless negotiator who liked to play the field. He has laughed in the faces of his male friends who settled down. After a life-threatening injury, he questions his way of life. He eventually settles down with Jodie.

Jodie Miller-Harris (nee Miller): Owns a spa in Invertary and runs a top-secret shelter for abused women. She has several martial arts black belts and is married to Mitch.

Joe Barone: Grunt's best friend. The ex-marine of American-Italian heritage has moved to London to be part of the new Benson Security office. Married to Julia.

Julia Barone (nee Collins): Julia is painfully shy—to the point of phobic behavior. She's also an organizational genius, and when she lost her previous job, she was snapped up by Lake Benson to work for him. She's currently office manager for the new London office. Her first task was to fill the building with large plants, so she'd have plenty of places to hide. She's married to Joe.

Rachel Ford-Talbot: Rachel was Harry's only friend in university and helped him set up his software business. She lives in London, is a terrible snob who comes from serious money, and a bitch—most of the time. She's one of the owners of Benson Security.

Ryan Granger: Ex-UK army, Ryan now works for Lake. He's a bit of a player with a dodgy sense of humor. He moved to London to work in the new Benson Security office but spends most of his free time clubbing.

Helen and Andrew McInnes: Josh's parents. They rekindled their love in Invertary castle and are now traveling the world. Andrew likes to think he's an expert on women.

Callum McKay: Ex-SAS soldier, one of the owners of Benson Security, and manager of the London office. He's bad-tempered, has two prosthetic legs, and adores his family. He's married to Isobel and has adopted her two kids, Jack and Sophie.

Isobel McKay (nee Sinclair): The eldest of the four

Sinclair sisters. She became a single mum at sixteen; then her later marriage, which resulted in another child, crumpled. She lived in a tiny town in the Mull of Kintyre until she met Callum and moved to London. She has two children, Jack (sixteen) and Sophie (three).

Agnes Sinclair: The second oldest of the sisters. She's been studying part time, while working, to get her degree in hotel management. She's the most capable and bad-tempered of the sisters.

Donna Stewart (nee Sinclair): The third Sinclair sister. Donna is a gifted illustrator who worked as house-keeper for the artist, Duncan Stewart, who owned Kintyre Mansion for years. She's now married to Duncan.

Duncan Stewart: A widowed artist who owns Kintyre Mansion and who's married to Donna.

Mairi McKenzie (nee Sinclair): The youngest Sinclair sister. She runs a matchmaking business that specializes in finding partners for geeky men.

Keir McKenzie: Mechanic who's engaged to Mairi.

Morag McKay: Invertary local who owns the bakery and makes great pies. She also runs the local morality society and likes to stage protests. She's one of Betty McLeod's arch nemeses.

About the Author

I'm a Scot, living in New Zealand and married to a Dutch man. I write contemporary romance with a humorous bent – this is mainly due to the fact I have an odd sense of humour and can't keep it out of anything I do! If I wasn't a writer, I'd like to be Buffy the Vampire Slayer, or Indiana Jones. Unfortunately, both these roles have already been filled. Which may be a good thing as I have no fighting skills, wouldn't know a precious relic if it hit me in the face and have an aversion to blood. When I'm not living in my head, I'm a mother to two kids, several pet sheep, one dog, four cats, three alpacas, two miniature horses, eight guinea pigs and an escape artist chicken.

Also by Janet Elizabeth Henderson

Thank you for reading my work.

If you enjoyed it, I hope you'll write a review. I love to hear what readers think. For information about upcoming books **sign up to receive my newsletter.** Or you can visit my **website** and **Facebook page** for news about my books.

Invertary, Scottish Highlands (Romantic Comedy)

Lingerie Wars, Invertary Book 1

Goody Two Shoes, Invertary Book 2

Magenta Mine, Invertary Book 3

Calamity Jena, Invertary Book 4

Bad Boy, Invertary Book 5

Here comes the Rainne again, Invertary Book 6

Caught, Invertary Book 7

Benson's Boys (Romantic Suspense)

Reckless, Book 1

Relentless, Book 2

Rage, Book 3

Ransom, Book 4

Rich, Book 5

Sinclair Sister Trilogy (Romantic Comedy)

Can't Tie Me Down! Book 1

Can't Stop the Feeling, Book 2

Can't Buy Me Love, Book 3

Red Zone (Paranormal Romance)

<u>Red Zone, Book 1</u>

<u>Red Awakening, Book 2</u>

Other Books (Contemporary Romance)

<u>Mad Love, London Book 1</u>

<u>Laura's Big Break, London Book 2</u>

<u>The Davina Code</u>